# MAIN STREET
## Home Front Hero

*Other* **MAIN STREET** *Books by*
**Susan E. Kirby**
*from Avon Camelot*

LEMONADE DAYS
HOME FOR CHRISTMAS

McLean, Illinois, where author SUSAN E. KIRBY lives, is remembered by her husband as a military corridor during World War II. HOME FRONT HERO was sparked by his recollections of troop convoys bivouacking in the pasture behind his childhood home. The hospitality "our boys" received along America's Main Street reflects through the eyes of a child the unity and patriotic fervor of a nation.

# MAIN STREET
## Home Front Hero

# SUSAN E. KIRBY

AN AVON CAMELOT BOOK

MAIN STREET: HOME FRONT HERO is an original publication of Avon Books. This work has never before appeared in book form. Any similarity to actual persons or events is purely coincidental.

AVON BOOKS
A division of
The Hearst Corporation
1350 Avenue of the Americas
New York, New York 10019

For Ronnie

# One

The beam of a passing truck slipped through Nick Kelsey's window. Light spilled across his bed and crawled up the wall. It tiptoed over little Charlie, then caught the curtains dancing with the breeze as it tripped back out over the sill.

From Midway Truck Stop came the smell of diesel fuel and fried chicken. Dew-soaked clover in the meadow sweetened the air. There was the scent of honeysuckle, too. It vined up Mama's clothesline pole. The other end of the line was anchored to the house and creaked beneath the weight of the rugs left hanging. A barn owl screeched. A car rushed by. A heavy freight train lumbered past, too loud for other sounds. Nick's eyes drifted shut. As the noise of the train faded, he was nearly asleep.

*C-r-e-e-c-h!*

Nick shot up in bed. "Mama?"

No answer.

He clutched his pillow and called again. How could

1

Mama sleep so soundly? Breathless, he listened hard and counted. One. Five. Ten. Nothing. Not even a cricket chirp.

Then it came again! Magnified by night's stillness, the creak stood out like a hymn book dropped in church. Nick stumbled out of bed. He felt his way across the landing to his mother's room. "Mama? Mama, wake up! Someone's on the back porch."

"Oh, Nick . . ." she began.

There was no mistaking the disbelief in her sleepy voice. Nick insisted, "There is! I heard the boards squeak."

"It's probably just the wind. Or maybe Gram's come home early."

"She'd use the front door. She'd be in and up the stairs by now."

"You sure she's not?"

Nick made his way to the lamp table at the top of the landing. He groped for the matches, struck one, and touched it to the lamp wick. The scent of smoldering lamp oil burned his throat. He hurried into the bedroom Gram Kelsey shared with his younger sister, Rebecca. Becca was alone in the room. She blinked and rubbed the sleep from her eyes.

"What's going on?"

"Shh!"

"What's wrong?"

"Stop talking so loud!" Nick jumped as Mama touched his shoulder.

"It sounds pretty quiet to me. Could it have been a dream?"

In the yard below, Wolf barked. A deep, vicious bark, it made a believer out of Mama. She urged them across the landing to Nick's room. "Stay in here with Charlie."

Mama rushed back to her room. She reappeared an instant later, dwarfed by his father's shotgun. At the top of the stairs, she dropped a shell into the chamber. She turned, thin lipped, as she warned, "You aren't to come down no matter what, hear?"

In the dim, shadowy light, Rebecca's eyes were as big as knotholes. "I'm scared, Mama! Don't go down!"

Mama motioned for her to hush. She started down the lamp-lit stairs. Her long robe trailed after her.

Nick's belly was a mass of wiggling snakes. Rebecca pulled him toward Charlie's crib. She patted the sleeping baby and whispered in a quivery voice, "It'll be all right. Mama's checking."

Nick itched from the inside out. He ran nervous fingers through his black hair. He shouldn't have let Mama go down there alone. "I better go see—"

"Mama said stay put!"

Nick wrenched his arm free. His pulse beat something fierce as he edged one foot forward. He crept silently toward the stairs. Becca slipped along behind him. Her breath tickled his neck.

"She said not to—"

"Hush, I can't hear!"

"Don't go! Don't leave Charlie and me here alone!"

"Shh!" Nick hissed.

The stairs were cool against his bare toes. He edged down one step, two steps, then stopped to listen. His nerves were tightly strung, keenly sensitive. It seemed as though he could feel the very grain of the wood beneath his feet.

Rebecca was on the step above him. She pressed so

3

close he couldn't tell where his trembling stopped and hers began. A sharp crack rang out. A thud followed. Nick's heart slammed violently against his chest as Becca cried out, "She shot him! Mama shot him!"

Nick tore down the stairs, Becca riding his back all the way.

# Two

The overhead light glinted off the steel barrel of the gun where it rested on the kitchen table. Maggie Campbell Kelsey, slim, short of stature, and quick to take issue, swung around as Nick and Rebecca bounded in. "What are you two doing down here?"

Nick raced right past her and out the back door. The porch was empty except for Gram's broom and a discarded grocery crate. He wheeled around in the open doorway. "Where is he? Did he get away?"

"I didn't see anyone," Mama said shortly.

"We heard you shoot!" cried Rebecca.

"I bumped into the table and knocked off a pop bottle."

"But I heard him hit the floor!" Nick exclaimed.

"That was me." Mama rubbed a skinned elbow, her voice growing more flinty by the second. "Someone left their marbles out."

"They're not mine." Becca backed away quickly.

Nick darted the scattered marbles a guilty glance. "I forgot."

"Just like you forgot that I told you to stay upstairs?"

"We thought you needed us."

"We wanted to help," Becca chimed in.

Eyes flashing, Mama set them straight in a hurry. "If your daddy can take on Hitler, rest assured I can handle a porch prowler. So long as you two are safely upstairs, that is, and not in the line of fire!"

Ashamed in the face of her spunk, Nick mumbled, "Sorry, Mama."

"Very well, then." Her voice softened a fraction. "Becca, pick up the bottle. Nick, get your marbles."

Nick crammed his marbles into their muslin drawstring pouch. Whoever had been on the porch had fled or Wolf would still be barking. Half collie, half German shepherd, Wolf was protective to a fault.

Mama took the bottle from Becca. "Go on back to bed, now."

"Are you coming?" A trace of fear lingered in Becca's voice.

"I'll be up as soon as I've checked the basement." Mama's tone gentled even further.

"I'll get the lamp," Nick said quickly.

Mama offered no objections. The basement, like the second floor, did not yet have electric lights. They'd moved into the old house soon after bombs were dropped on Pearl Harbor in December of '41. An Oklahoma farmboy turned carpenter, Nick's father, Robert Kelsey, had worked on the house in his spare time. He'd just finished wiring the downstairs when his draft number came up. Now, their only link to their father was letters. The news was old and sketchy, for "leaks lost lives." His last letter had arrived five days after D-Day, and removed all doubt—he'd been with the Allied forces landing in Normandy. Like all V-mail, the letter had been written on a single sheet, photographed, then reduced in size by the postal service to conserve space. Certain phrases were censored, but Nick was reassured by Dad's strong handwriting and the news that he was well. But it'd been four days now since they'd received his letter, with no further word.

Nick came back with the lamp. He set it down for Mama, then picked up the gun. "I'll carry it for you."

"You'll do no such thing. Put it down!"

Nick hesitated, savoring the weight of the gun in his hands. To him Normandy was a vague somewhere, "over there"—a dangerous somewhere. The waiting, as the Allied invasion battered away at the Nazis, was making Mama edgy. Which accounted for her considerably shortened wick. So thinking, he swallowed a protest and returned the gun to the table.

"That's better," said Mama.

A musty odor rose up to meet them as she opened the basement door. She lifted the lamp, lighting their way. Nick's heart picked up its pace. But Mama marched down without hesitation. Nick followed her past the coal bin and around bundled newspapers, boxes of junk metal, cast-off pans and empty tins they were saving for the next scrap drive. There was a can of grease they were saving; the Scouts were collecting grease for the war effort.

In the storage room a wall of shelves sagged beneath the weight of home-canned fruits and vegetables from Gram's Victory garden. The lamplight exposed nothing but hairy spiders lurking in the damp, dark corners. Mama checked the cellar door leading outside. It was securely bolted.

7

After a thorough search, Mama started back up to the kitchen. She covered a yawn. "So much for intruders. Let's get some sleep."

In all of his ten years, Nick couldn't remember ever being more tired. But his thoughts wouldn't be still. He turned on his side. The lights of a passing convoy repeated the path across his room. The drone of the engines identified them as military vehicles.

Living alongside Route 66 in western Missouri, Nick watched by day the movement of troops and goods for the war. Occasionally, a convoy would stop and camp overnight in the pasture. The road itself seemed a rich, winding mystery. You could never tell what would come down it. Or who it would draw away.

There were dangers too, living so close to the road. Sometimes vagrants came to their door, men down on their luck with tattered clothes, worn-out shoes, weathered, unshaven faces, and unwashed bodies. Some offered to do chores in exchange for a meal. Some wanted a drink from the pump or asked to sleep in the barn out in the back pasture.

Gram Kelsey and Mama never sent them away hungry. But they wouldn't let anyone spend the night in the barn. It was leased to the veterinarian, Dr. Carbury. Doc lived across the street. When asked, he also refused permission.

But some didn't bother asking. Sometimes, Nick found matted-down beds of straw in the loft. He didn't mention it to Mama. It was the sort of thing he felt certain Dad would have kept from her.

Nick reached for the framed picture resting on the night table. It was too dark to make out his father. But he had an image in his mind: Dad dressed in his uniform, grave and unsmiling.

Nick closed his eyes, thoughts reeling back to a day last summer. He'd been on the back porch, pulling burrs out of Wolf's thick fur. His father, home on furlow before shipping out, had joined him on the step. Together, they'd watched a convoy pass on the highway.

"I wish I was older. I'd go with you, Dad. *Pop, pop, pow!*" He'd aimed the broom, staring down it as if it were the barrel of a gun.

His father's face had lengthened. He'd heaved a deep sigh. Nick hadn't understood, then, how long the separation would be or how anxious. Excited by the olive-drab jeeps, busses, and trucks, he had slung the broom over his shoulder and marched across the yard, singing:

*Kaiser Bill went up the hill to take a peep at France,*
*Kaiser Bill came down the hill with bullets in his pants.*

"Wrong war," his father had murmured.

"Gram sings it to Charlie."

"Yes." His father's head had dropped.

Wolf's grooming forgotten, Nick had pressed his shoulder against his father's hard-muscled arm. A callused hand closed over his knee. "It's got Gram thinking old thoughts," his father'd said quietly.

Nick could guess at some of Gram's thoughts, for Grandpa Kelsey had lost a leg in that other war. "Old Hickory," Grandpa had called his wooden leg. And once he'd told Nick with a wink that termites were to blame for his limp. But never, until the day he died, had he talked about the battle where he'd lost his leg.

Except to Gram. Her eyes flooded yet at the mention of it.

"She's a brave woman, your gram. But she isn't getting any younger," his father had spoken over his thoughts. "Help her all you can."

"I will."

"Mind your mother and don't fight with your sister."

Nick had crossed his fingers and promised.

"Start up the truck every now and again."

"I'll grease it and watch the oil and keep it running real good," Nick had promised.

"You do that," his father had said.

Nick had nearly popped, so proud was he of the confidence in his father's voice. But then, why not? Nick *was* a fair hand at mechanics, thanks in part to his other grandfather, Grandpa Dave. He ran a gas station in Oklahoma along Route 66, the same highway that passed Nick's house. Mama and Dad had met at that station a long time ago. They'd courted and married and moved to Missouri shortly after Becca was born. Gram Sophie and Grandpa Dave and Uncle Jeremiah came to visit at least twice a year. Nick's family returned the visits now and again, traveling 66 to Oklahoma.

Nick had ventured a glance at his father's firmly set chin and asked boldly, "Can I drive it?"

A faint curve had relaxed his mouth. "A turn or two around the meadow wouldn't do any harm. As long as your mother's looking on. But don't dare take it out on the hard road. Henry Gibbs'll slap you in jail so fast it'll make your head spin."

Henry Gibbs was the town constable. "I'd never do that," Nick'd promised.

"As long as you understand," his father'd said.

"While I'm gone, you're man of the house. You can handle that, can't you?"

Nick's chest had swelled with pride as he'd nodded and stretched out his hand. His father had shaken it, as if to seal a solemn pact. Ever since then, sparing Mama worry and knowing all about Dad's gun and how to change a fuse when the lights went out was just part and parcel of filling Dad's shoes. As was keeping the old truck in good running order with an occasional drive around the meadow.

Course he'd fussed with Becca some and he hadn't always minded Mama and he'd let her go down those stairs alone. Mama was spunky, but she was still a woman and in need of protection. So thinking, Nick slipped the picture beneath the tattered edges of the sheet and held it close. Next time, he would not let his father down.

The sensation of pain awakened Nick. The sharp corner of the picture frame was gouging him. He rolled over and rubbed the tender spot in his side.

Early morning sunlight peeked through the half-drawn shades. Across the room, Charlie was trying to get out of his wet pajamas. Nick helped him finish the job.

He pulled one of his own T-shirts over Charlie's tousled black curls. Charlie toddled over to the picture lying on Nick's bed.

"Da-da." Charlie bounced on the balls of his feet. He gave the picture a sloppy kiss. His pudgy fingers traced squiggly circles on the glass. "Da-da."

"Yes, that's Da-da. And look how you've smeared the glass." Nick wiped the glass dry with the corner of his sheet and returned the picture to the table.

11

He carried Charlie downstairs and out to the privy where he demonstrated the purpose of the gaping hole. Every morning for a week now, Nick'd given the same lesson. Not quite two, Charlie enjoyed the sessions. He danced and talked gibberish and clapped his hands in delight. But so far, the only thing he'd sent down the hole was Gram's garden catalog.

Nick's belly was rumbling. "Maybe tomorrow," he said. He led the way out, then latched the privy door. Charlie didn't like the dewy grass. He curled his toes and whined.

"It's damp, that's all. It won't hurt you," Nick said.

Charlie's bottom lip quivered. Nick was about to pick him up when Gram Kelsey came around the side of the house. She'd moved here from Oklahoma shortly after Grandpa Kelsey died of tuberculosis. Just home from her night shift at the telephone office, she yawned and scratched her gray head. "What's got into Charlie?"

"He doesn't like getting his feet wet."

"Well, God love him!" Gram nudged Nick aside. "Let me at those sweet feet."

There was a pin shaped into a letter *V* decorating the collar of Gram's dress. It stood for victory. She'd worn it since the day Daddy left. Charlie pick-picked at the red, white, and blue rhinestones as Gram brushed his feet. The lines of her face curved into a smile as she dried his feet and kissed his fingers. "That better, angel?"

Nick was used to Gram going soft over Charlie. Mama and Rebecca were nearly as bad. Truth was, Charlie'd carved a special place in his heart, too.

Following Gram to the house, Nick said, "We had a prowler last night."

12

"A prowler?" She swung around. Her faded blue eyes narrowed attentively as Nick nodded.

"I heard someone on these boards here. Wolf heard 'im too. He barked fit to raise the dead." Nick trooped up the steps behind her.

"Iris mentioned he woke her. You know what a light sleeper she is," Gram said.

Iris Clark, the nosiest woman on earth, lived next door. She relieved Gram at the telephone office. There were Gram Kelsey and Iris and Mama and two part-time ladies. Among them, they manned the switchboard day and night.

"Did she say anything about hearing our porch creak?" Nick marched across the porch. The sagging boards protested beneath his trampling steps. "It sounded just like that."

"No, not a word."

"We could have been robbed, Gram!"

"Imagination's a good tool, child, as long as you don't get carried away." Gram patted him on the head and let herself into the house.

She didn't believe him! Nick plunked down and kicked his bare heels against the back of the step. A chip of dried paint lodged itself in his foot. He reached down to remove it, then stopped, noticing a red stain on the step. It was his job to catch fryers and boilers, wring necks, and lob off heads. If he dripped blood on the steps, Mama saw to it he scrubbed them clean. But they hadn't eaten chicken all week. Puzzled, he examined the stain closer. It sure *looked* like blood. The screen door whined behind him.

"Don't forget to feed Wolf," Gram reminded.

Half turning, Nick asked, "Gram, did you or Mama butcher a chicken yesterday?"

She wagged her head and turned away, saying, "Sounds tasty, though. Maybe for Sunday dinner."

The door banged shut again. Nick ran his finger over the splotch. It was dry, but it wasn't that faded brown color blood turned over time. He mashed his lips together, thinking. Yesterday, he'd sat right where he was sitting now, sharpening his knife on a bit of broken crockery. He was certain the splotch hadn't been there then. If it *was* blood, it was fresh. The more closely he examined it, the more certain he became.

Despite the warmth of the rising sun, a chill passed through Nick. His heart pounded like a hammer on a fifty-five-gallon steel drum. Could the blood have been left by the would-be intruder?

# Three

Charlie toddled out the back door, interrupting Nick's racing thoughts. Mama chased him down, his shoes in her hand. She had dark circles under her eyes, and her flowered robe was buttoned crooked. But she smiled as she caught Charlie up in her arms and hung on tight when he tried to break free. Nick slid to one side, making room for them on the step.

Mama sank down beside him, Charlie still squirming in her arms. "Careful with that knife, Nick. What's that you're doing?"

"Examining clues." Nick picked at the dried blood with his pocketknife.

"Clues?"

Nick nodded and pointed out the blood. "The way I figure it, whoever was prowling around out here last night must have been injured."

"Hmm," said Mama, the way she did when her attention strayed in the middle of a conversation. She tied Charlie's shoes, then patted Nick's knee absently. "You boys hungry?"

It was as if Wolf's barking in the night had never happened! Frustrated, Nick stretched his bare toes toward the grass and plucked the head off a dandelion. Charlie slid off Mama's lap, backed down the stairs, and leaned close to examine the beheaded weed.

"Mama? Do you suppose it was a robber?" asked Nick in a hush.

"Set Wolf to barking? A cat, more than likely. You know how he hates cats."

A cat could not make the porch floor creak! "It wasn't a cat. I'm sure of that."

"I can make hot cereal. Or would you rather have eggs?" She kept an eye on Charlie.

"Cereal." Nick wished she'd quit changing the subject.

"No, no, Charlie! Not in your mouth. Get him, Nick!"

Nick snatched the dandelion away before Charlie could eat it. Charlie stiffened as he picked him up and let out a yell. "Big boy like Charlie, pitching a fit? Big enough to make a trip to the privy. Hush now, and tell Mama where we went this morning. Go on, tell Mama." Nick coaxed him out of his tantrum.

Charlie crawled into Mama's lap again and blurted a bit of gibberish.

"The privy?" said Mama, making her eyes go wide. "My, my. That *is* a big boy. How'd you do? How'd he do, Nick?"

"He's trying," said Nick tactfully. But he rolled his eyes when Charlie wasn't looking and whispered, "He couldn't make water with a garden hose."

Mama chuckled and combed Nick's untidy curls with her fingers. "He's still a baby."

"He's almost two."

"Yes, and you're pushin' him, just like Aunt Susan used to do to Uncle Jeremiah. There Jere was, five years younger, and always reaching to keep up with her."

Nick smiled, thinking fondly of Aunt Susan. She and her brother, Razz, had been orphaned when Mama was just a girl back in Illinois. Razz had moved in with a preacher there in Shirley and Gram Sophie had made a home for Susan. After Grandpa Dave had moved the family to Oklahoma, they opened their home to another orphan, that being Jeremiah. Aunt Susan was married now, with a little girl about Charlie's age. And just two weeks ago, Jeremiah had graduated from high school and joined the Army.

Mama stirred Nick from his thoughts, saying, as she came to her feet, "Keep an eye on Charlie while I dress, then get a fire going in the stove."

Nick fed Wolf and gave him fresh water. He lay papers, corncobs, and coal, then snatched Charlie back from the coal bucket. "Oh, no you don't. You'll be black, head to foot. Here, how about this?"

Nick gave Charlie a corncob to play with. He pumped a bucket full of water at the sink and filled the stove reservoir. The grate was warm when Mama returned. She had a *V* pin on her collar, too.

"Somebody crashed on dead man's curve last night," she said as she tied an apron over her dress. "Every Tom, Dick, and Harry called to find out what'd happened. Gram was at the switchboard all night. Didn't get a bit of rest. Be real quiet and let her sleep."

"Who was in the accident? Anybody we know?" Nick asked.

Mama wagged her head. "It was a couple from Tulsa

17

headed for St. Louis. Henry Gibbs drove them to County Hospital.''

''Were they hurt bad?''

''The man had a broken leg. He passed out from the pain. The woman was dazed. She went on about a third passenger—a soldier boy, she claimed. But there was only the two of them in the car according to Henry.''

''That so? Wonder if they've hauled the car away yet.''

''What car?'' asked Becca, joining them.

Nick listened carefully as Mama repeated the story Gram had relayed to her. Odd, that the third passenger had disappeared before help came.

After breakfast, Nick set off to see what he could learn about the wreck.

''Wait for me!'' Rebecca called. She caught up with him in front of Dr. Carbury's house. They waded through uncut weeds and grass in the empty lot next to the veterinarian's, then crossed a side street to E. Z.'s Mechanic Shop. E. Z.'s faced Route 66. On the other side of the road was Midway Truck Stop. Much of E. Z.'s business came to him from there.

The car, a late-model Studebaker, was a sorry sight. The glass in the windshield was broken, and the front end was stove in. E. Z. waved from the open door.

''What'd they hit?'' Nick called.

''Signpost.'' The potbellied proprietor came out to join the children. He pointed down the road a block and a half. Midway Truck Stop's billboard had stood on that spot just a day ago. ''They were coming off the curve there. Ended up over in that field. Made kindling out of that heavy post.''

Rebecca wrinkled her freckled nose. "They must have been going too fast."

E. Z. spat in the dirt. "The curve, then the stop sign make a bad combination. Folks aren't used to having to stop on 66."

"Mama says they took a man and a woman to the hospital," said Becca.

"From what I hear, they should pull through okay." E. Z. hitched up his trousers.

Nick circled the car, surveying the damage and wondering about that third passenger. He stuck his head through a side window. "What's that, poked under the seat?"

The unshaven middle-aged mechanic craned his sunburned neck and peered through the open window.

"Let me see." Becca nudged in beside him.

Nick tried the door, but it wouldn't open.

"I'll get it," said Becca.

E. Z. gave her a boost. She scrambled through the car window and came out seconds later with something green clutched in her hand.

"An overseas hat! There was a soldier with them, all right," said E. Z.

"Is there a name inside?" Nick asked.

E. Z. turned the hat in his hand. "Nope, but there's the letter *P* and four numbers."

Puzzled, Nick scratched his head. "Wonder what became of him?"

E. Z. shrugged. "Must have walked away from it. You'd think he'd stick around to see about the other folks, though. Peculiar, ain't it?"

Becca tugged at Nick's sleeve. "Let's go tell the constable."

"I thought he'd be along by now." E. Z. took a gander at his timepiece, then looked up the street. A note of impatience crept into his tone. "Wonder what's keeping him?"

"You already called the constable?" asked Nick.

"Had Iris ring him as soon as I opened up this morning. There was money missing out of my cash drawer."

Nick caught a startled breath. "You were *robbed*?"

The mechanic nodded. "A few dollars in change. That's all I ever leave in the drawer at night."

Eyes bugging wide, Becca cried, "We could've been robbed, too! Somebody was messing on our porch last night."

"I heard and woke Mama," said Nick.

"Then Wolf started barking and scared whoever it was away." Becca shared the telling.

"Guess I oughta get me a dog like Wolf," said E. Z. "That critter's just plain mean."

"Not with us, he isn't." Becca defended their pet.

"How'd the thief get in the station? Did he bust down a door?" Nick asked.

E. Z. rubbed his bristly chin. "No. No sign of forced entry. Junior closed up last night. He swears he double-checked the doors. But that boy gets in a hurry sometimes. He isn't as careful as he ought to be."

Junior was E. Z.'s teenage son. E. Z. closed the cover of his watch and glanced up the street again. "You kids probably ought to tell Constable Gibbs what happened at your house last night. Then see if you can't hurry him along."

Nobody hurried Henry Gibbs. He was a gruff, towering man who moved as he pleased. Still, Nick agreed it was a good idea to pay him a visit. He raced Rebecca toward the middle of town. At the main crossing the flagman was ambling out onto the railroad tracks. He took out his pocket watch and gazed up the tracks.

Becca said, "We're looking for Constable Gibbs. Have you seen him, Mr. L'Angelo?"

"His car's sitting in front of the jail. Someone in trouble?"

"We'll tell you later!" Nick promised, off and running again.

Rebecca put up a good race. But Nick beat her to the jail by a good three yards. Henry Gibbs was lolling back in a chair, asleep at his desk. His eyes jerked open as Rebecca clattered in after Nick, panting and complaining.

"No fair, you had a head start!"

"Did not."

"Did too."

"Cut it out, or I'll lock up the both of you for disturbing the peace." Mr. Gibbs's heavy feet came down off the desk with a thud. He stood up and stretched his tall rawboned frame. There were dark pouches under his eyes. He looked as if he hadn't slept in a week—and cross with it.

Nick shuffled his feet. "Sorry we woke you, Mr. Gibbs. E. Z. sent us to see what was keeping you."

Constable Gibbs rubbed his bleary eyes, grumbling, "Since when is three forty-five in change an emergency? Bet you a chocolate bar Junior's done something with it."

"I don't know," hedged Nick. "We could have had a break-in too if it weren't for Wolf."

Mr. Gibbs listened intently as Nick related the incident.

"Prowler woke your mama, too, did he?"

"No. I heard and woke her," said Nick.

"Then Wolf barked and scared him off," Becca chimed in.

"Hmmph," said the constable. Attention shifting, he beckoned toward the cap in Nick's hand, asking, "What's that you got there?"

Too late, Nick remembered Mr. Gibbs didn't put much stock in the testimony of children. Disappointed in having last night's scare so easily dismissed, he passed the cap to the constable. "We found this soldier hat in the car that wrecked last night."

"E. Z. says it's an overseas hat," offered Becca.

Constable Gibbs examined the inside of the hat with his long, big, square-tipped fingers. " 'P one seven nine eight.' That'd be the first initial of his last name and the last four digits of his identification number." He stroked his whiskered chin. "Where in tarnation do you suppose that soldier disappeared to?"

A sudden thought rang like a bell in Nick's head: What if it *wasn't* a prowler last night? It could have been the soldier, come to get help when Wolf scared him off.

Nick opened his mouth, then thought better of it. Could be he had it all wrong. And besides, Mr. Gibbs'd been awful quick to dismiss last night's account. Best have a look for himself before he went airing his theories again. But it was worrisome, thinking of the splotch of blood on the porch. If it *had* been the soldier, he must be injured.

\* \* \*

"Maybe the fella's furlow was nearly up. He could've hitched another ride and went on his way, rather'n risk being listed as AWOL," speculated Mr. L'Angelo moments later when Nick and Rebecca returned to the crossing.

"Absent without leave," Nick answered Becca's blank look.

"Commanding officers take a real dim view of that," said Mr. L'Angelo.

"I guess that *could* explain it," said Becca.

Nick could tell by her furrowed brow she wasn't altogether satisfied, even as she went on to tell about E. Z.'s missing change. A car approached the tracks. Mr. L'Angelo let it pass, then went out onto the tracks and held up his stop sign.

"Train's coming. Get clear of the tracks, kids."

Nick had spent enough time in the flagman's hut that he was familiar with the schedule. "It's the mail train, isn't it?"

Mr. L'Angelo nodded his white head. "And right on time, too."

Nick and Becca hurried on. Rebecca ducked into the station to see if anyone inside had seen an injured soldier. Nick continued on. Up ahead, the mail pouch hung from a post alongside the tracks. Mr. Ashland the postman stood nearby, waiting for the incoming mail. Maybe there'd be a letter from Dad. Nick's heart quickened with hope.

The train came on without slowing. It was full of soldiers. Up track, Rebecca and the station manager's children were waving. Down track, the postman gave a smart salute.

Nick waved too. He'd been lifting his hand to soldiers

even before his daddy went off to war. Since the day Newt Jackson came home, in fact. The *Abraham Lincoln* was a streamline. She and the *Ann Rutledge* were the Gulf Mobile & Ohio's speedsters. They passed the little towns like Sweet Clover without even slowing. But that day, the *Abe Lincoln* had stopped.

All of Sweet Clover had turned out on the platform. The women had cried. Some of the men, too, as the flag-draped casket was lifted down off the train. That day, Newt wasn't just Herb and Birdie Jackson's boy. That day, Newt was the whole town's boy. The whole country's. Thinking of Newt and thinking of his daddy in the same twitch of an eye made Nick's stomach hurt.

A man on the train held a hooked rod. With it, he reached out and snagged up the bag of outgoing mail. At almost the same moment, a canvas mail pouch was flung from the train. It landed a few feet from Mr. Ashland. But it'd be an hour or so before the postman would have the letters sorted.

"Have you seen a soldier around town, Mr. Ashland?" Nick called to the postman.

Mr. Ashland said that he hadn't. He listened to what Nick had to say and promised to pass the news along at the post office.

Rebecca caught up with Nick. They walked home, planning to search for the soldier until time to get the mail. But Mama was ready to leave for the first half of her split shift at the telephone office. She worked nine to one, then went back at five and worked until nine at night. Watching Mama pin on her hat, Nick withheld his private theory about the soldier being on the porch last night and told her instead about E. Z. being robbed.

24

"Junior probably took it. It'd be just like him to help himself," said Mama.

Mama and Henry Gibbs and most of the town were of the opinion Edgar Zeke, Junior, was out of hand. Despite the shortages brought on by the war, Junior always had fuel for his '34 Pontiac coupe. It made Mama fume to see him drive past the house. She, and nearly everyone else in town, did errands on foot. It was their patriotic duty to conserve fuel for the war effort.

"You two keep Charlie out of Iris Clark's yard. He walked all over her marigolds yesterday." Mama interrupted his thoughts. "Nick, when you finish your other chores, hoe Gram's garden. Becca, hang out the clothes I washed this morning."

"But we want to look for the soldier," Rebecca complained.

"That's Henry Gibbs's job," said Mama. "I'll be home at one. Then you'll be free to play."

*Play!* Nick stood tall and straight. "This is important, Mama. He could be hurt."

"Posh! He's caught another ride, that's all. Take care you don't wake Gram. And don't let Charlie wake her either."

Mama passed Charlie into his care. She hooked her purse over her arm and hurried off to work.

# Four

Rebecca picked up the clothespin Charlie had scattered on the kitchen floor. "Let's do our chores quick just in case Gram wakes up. Then we can look for the soldier."

Nick had spent nights at the telephone office with Gram. There was a bed in the back room. When there weren't any calls coming in, Gram got a fair amount of sleep. But last night had not been one of those nights.

"Bet she sleeps all day. Course we could look anyway." He shot Rebecca a quick glance. When Mama was at work, they weren't to leave the yard without Gram's permission except to get the mail.

"What about Charlie?" asked Rebecca.

"We'd have to take him with us."

Rebecca chewed her lip a moment. "We could pull him along in the wagon. If Mama finds out, we'll say we were giving Charlie a ride to the post office."

"If the soldier was lying right out in plain sight, someone would have found him by now," Nick reasoned. "A wagon won't go the places we have to look."

Becca sniffed. "Do you have a better idea?"

"Yeah. You watch Charlie and I'll go look."

"Go on then. But if Mama should ask, don't expect me to cover for you." Becca twisted out to the clothesline. She snatched a wet diaper from the basket.

Nick sighed. Making her mad wasn't helping a bit. Maybe if he shared his theory with her, she'd cool down and be reasonable. So thinking, Nick called her back and showed her the blood on the step. "I'm sure it wasn't there yesterday."

"You think it was the soldier? On our porch? Last night? It was *him* making Wolf bark?" Becca pieced together Nick's suspicions.

"That's one possibility. Either that or whoever robbed E. Z. was trying to break into our house," he added.

"Henry Gibbs didn't seem to think it was a robbery. Neither did Mama," Becca was quick to remind him. "Though if it *was* a robbery . . ." She paused and blinked, wide-eyed. "Nick, could he be a soldier and a robber, too?"

It was an ugly thought. Nick felt disloyal to every man in uniform just for entertaining it. After all, the soldiers were fighting to make Hitler give back what didn't belong to him. Stealing was stealing, whether it was a country or change from E. Z.'s cash box. He couldn't feature his dad or Newt Jackson or any other soldier stooping so low. "I don't think so." He answered Becca's question.

She looked so relieved, he knew she didn't want to think it either. Nevertheless, she reasoned, "If it *was* him on our porch, he should have called for help."

"Maybe he was in shock. Maybe he didn't have the

strength to call for help. Person loses too much blood and—'' Nick zipped his finger across his throat.

Becca's shivered and relented. "Okay, okay! I'll watch Charlie. You go look. But don't be gone too long."

"You won't tell? Cross your heart?"

Becca crossed her heart and promised.

Nick hurried to Route 66. He walked through the ditches on either side of the road. He checked the abandoned blacksmith shop and the patches of weeds near the Midway Truck Stop, then took time out for a quick trip to the post office, only to find their postal box empty. No letter from Dad. Shrugging off his disappointment, Nick resumed his search, working his way through steep, weedy ditches skirting the railroad tracks. He was gone much longer than he'd intended. But he didn't find a trace of the missing soldier.

Becca shared his bewilderment. She ventured, "Maybe Mama's right. Maybe he caught another ride."

Nick got a hoe from the toolshed and went to work on Gram's Victory garden. He bypassed spent pea vines. A row of leafy carrot tops gave way to four rows of corn. He hoed carefully around the tender spikes. The sun had grown hot. Streams of sweat stung his eyes. He straightened his back. It was odd, but somehow he felt as though he were being watched.

He looked in the direction of Iris Clark's house. Iris had sharp eyes and a tongue to match. Mama even got put out with her sometimes, saying it was just like living next door to Miss Greer Tims back in Oklahoma. Nick didn't know about that, for Gram and Grandpa Tilton's neighbor, Miss Tims, had died sometime back and her house sat empty now. But if she'd been as big a trial

28

as Iris Clark, he was sorry for Mama and Aunt Susan. But today there wasn't so much as a stir of a curtain from Iris Clark's house.

Nick ate a raw green bean. He resumed chopping weeds. But the feeling persisted. It was rather like shooing a fly off your face, only to have it land on your arm. He leaned on his hoe and looked all about. There was nothing unusual to see. The sounds were all familiar, too: birds in the meadow, traffic passing on the road, Becca and Charlie in the yard. They were playing beneath blankets she'd draped over the line.

Mama came home at one. She fixed them a late lunch. While they ate, she related the news concerning the missing soldier.

"Henry Gibbs called County Hospital. The folks injured in that wreck last night said the soldier'd told them he'd been home on leave and was thumbing his way back to his base."

"Fort Leonard Wood?" guessed Nick.

"That's what they figured, anyway," said Mama.

Taking into account the direction the soldier'd been headed, it was a logical assumption. "Did Mr. Gibbs call the base?" he asked.

Mama nodded. "He gave them that number off the hat. They were going to try and track it down. See if the boy made it back all right."

"Becca and I want to look for him. Just in case he's still in town," Nick added quickly.

Mama rose to clear away the dishes, saying, "That's thoughtful of you, but I don't think it's necessary. Henry'll get a call from the Army this afternoon and the whole puzzle will be solved." Nick could not say what made him so certain she was mistaken.

After lunch, the children went out to the barn. Their father's pickup truck was parked in one end. Nearby was the tack room. Doc Carbury used it as a catchall for supplies, old records, and such. At the center of the barn was the stock pen. It doubled as Doc's large-animal surgery. There were iron rings on the floor where he secured the animals before operating.

Nick's own special place was a small room which had once been used for storing grain. While cleaning the place out, he'd found a scoop shovel with a broken handle. That's how his hideout had gotten the name the broken shovel.

"You can come in, too, if you want," said Nick, approaching the door to his hideout.

Becca wrinkled her nose. "It's too dusty. Let's go sit in Daddy's truck."

Nick raced her to the truck and slid into the driver's seat. Sitting there in the barn, with wisps of straw stringing down from the loft, Nick pretended he was driving around the meadow. Becca, who often rode with him, played the part of Mama. She planted her feet against the floorboards and braced a hand against the dashboard.

"Slow down." She assumed Mama's bossy tone. "We're warming the motor, not running a race! Watch that bump. Easy on the clutch. Scoot over here by me, Becca. Becca! Becca! Becca!"

Rebecca covered her eyes and slid down in the seat. She opened an eye and grinned, purposely provoking him with the reminder of the day she'd fallen out of the truck because of the faulty latch on the passenger door.

"That wasn't my fault," Nick protested.

"You were driving."

"Mama warned you. Anyway, I was barely moving."

"It didn't feel that way to me." Becca rolled her eyes, remembering.

Nick laughed in spite of himself. He'd slammed on the brakes and looked back that day to see her sprawled in a patch of young clover. She'd been rubbing her bottom, yelling, "Hey! Come back here!"

She'd looked so comical, Mama had laughed, too, once she was certain Becca wasn't hurt. Then she'd told them a story about her childhood in Illinois and how she and a neighbor boy named Ivan had gone for a wild ride in a Model-A Ford when the concrete on 66 was so new it was still curing. Bootleggers had chased them, and they'd ended up crashing. The very thought of it made Nick itch for adventure.

Becca wrote her name on the dust-coated dashboard. She scribbled it out then and sighed. "I wish I knew what'd become of that soldier."

Nick's thoughts turned back to the soldier, too. He said, "Let's ask Mama if we can take Wolf for a walk. We'll stop by the jail and take a look at the soldier's hat."

"What for?"

"So Wolf can smell it. Then we'll take him down to where the accident happened. Maybe he can pick up a scent."

Becca's brow furrowed. "Do you really think he can?"

31

"He hunts rabbits. So why wouldn't he be able to pick up a human trail?"

Becca appeared to be thinking it over. Nick reached past her. He opened the glove box and took out a rag, then jumped out and opened the hood. The last time he'd driven the truck, it had not run very smoothly. Puttering around in the meadow was no substitute for driving out on the open road. He daydreamed a moment about sneaking the truck out on the hard road and running her wide open—one hand on the wheel, elbow bent out the window, the wind in his face, sailing past fence posts sporting Burma-Shave signs. He tinkered a bit, then latched the hood and returned his attention to Becca.

"So do you want to or not?"

"I guess so," Becca jumped out of the truck. "You get Wolf on the walking strap and I'll run get permission."

Nick had made Wolf's strap himself from some old reins he'd found in the barn. The cobbler down the street had helped him with the stitching. He'd found it useful for things other than walking Wolf. If memory served, he'd left the strap in the broken shovel. There weren't any windows in his hideout. With the door closed, it was black as ink inside. He'd run the strap through a rafter knothole and hung a lantern from it.

The bottom of the door to his hideout was several feet off the floor. That was necessary, when the room had been used as a granary. Otherwise, the grain would have spilled out when the door was opened. Nick climbed up on a stack of boards. He reached for the piece of baling wire that held the door shut, then pulled his hand back and blinked. The wire was gone!

Maybe Dr. Carbury had helped himself and simply forgotten to replace it. Nick swung the narrow door open. He poked in his head. His skin prickled as if a cat had just licked him from head to toe.

He smelled cigarette smoke. And something else, too. A *human* smell! Gooseflesh chased down his arms. But he overcame his impulse to run. "Who's there?"

His words rang hollow and small. They faded and faded, until there was no sound left. Nick's eyes burned from trying to make out the black corners. Nothing stirred. Was he mistaken? Was the room empty?

Or was it his friend Billy Jones? Had he returned from Kentucky with the homegrown tobacco he'd bragged he'd be bringing from his grandpa's farm? Of course! A wave of relief went over Nick.

Now wasn't it just like Billy to have a little fun at his expense? Grinning, Nick hoisted himself up, braced a foot on the threshold, and leaped in. "You can't scare me, Billy," he hollered. "I know you're—"

His words were cut short as a hand closed over his mouth. A deep voice rumbled in his ear.

"Shut that door behind you, son, and don't make a sound."

# Five

Nick lurched for the door. Strong arms snatched him back. The last scrap of light disappeared as the granary door swung shut. His stifled cry filled the darkness.

"I'm not going to hurt you. I need a little help, that's all. Don't holler now, and I'll turn you loose." As good as his word, the man eased his grip on Nick.

Nick swallowed the impulse to scream. He stood trembling in silence. A match flared, a fleeting spark of light. In it Nick glimpsed a blood-smeared, unshaven cheek and a drab uniform. His fear evaporated. The injured soldier!

"Want me to run get Dr. Maxwell?" He spoke to the glowing tip of the cigarette.

"No, wait. It's not that simple."

"But you need help!"

"I'm banged up a bit, but I'm getting by."

"How bad are you hurt?"

"My ankle's swollen and sore. I've got some cuts and bruises, too. But I'll mend. What I really need is a bite to eat. That, and a little rest and a way back to my base. Will you help me?"

"If I can. Are you sure you don't want me to get the doctor?"

"Thanks, but I don't need him."

"What about the town constable? He's looked all over town for you."

The man made a tight sound in his throat. "Best not. Don't know if he's to be trusted."

The constable, trusted? Had the soldier bumped his head? Had he lost so much blood, he was confused? Or was he the robber, after all? Like a hot ember, the thought burned to be spoken. "You know anything about the break-in at E. Z.'s station?" Nick blurted.

"Who?"

"E. Z. The mechanic. Somebody took money from his cash box last night."

"A robbery? Oh, great! That's just what I need!" The man sounded dismayed. "Now I *know* I can't risk talking to the constable."

"Then it wasn't you?"

"No, of course not!"

"Then why're you hiding in our barn?" Nick pressed.

"I'm on a military mission, son. I can't say much about it, except that it's gone awry. But believe me, I never in my life took a dime that didn't belong to me."

"But you *were* in the car that was wrecked last night?"

"I'm afraid so. If you're willing to help, you can start by not asking questions," he said quietly. "The less you know, the less danger for both of us."

*Danger?* Nick's blood tingled. Was he with Army intelligence? A courier with secret information pursued

35

by Nazi spies? Why, this could be an adventure to match Mama's childhood flight from bootleggers!

Nick turned his head. Becca was calling him. "That's my sister. She's going to come looking."

The soldier waited for what seemed an eternity. The thickness of the cigarette smoke made Nick cough.

"All right, then," said the soldier at last. "But could you slip back out here later with something to eat? And some water, too. I need to soak my ankle."

"I'll do my best."

"Take care you don't arouse suspicion."

"Nick? Are you coming or not?" called Rebecca. Wolf began to bark. Nick ran outside to meet her.

"Mama said be back in half an hour. Did you find Wolf's walking strap?"

"No. We'll have to use the rope instead." Nick was careful as he hurried into the sunlight to keep his face turned away. If Becca suspected he had a secret, she'd push and prod at him like a pair of tweezers until finally the truth'd pop out. And that wouldn't do, would it?

Would it? The question rang in his mind as he pulled on a glove to keep Wolf's rope from burning his hand. They started down the slate sidewalk. Wolf walked with quiet dignity. Rebecca skipped along beside him. She made suggestions as to how to convince Constable Gibbs to let them borrow the hat.

Nick's head was too full of his own thoughts to listen. Could he really look after the soldier without anyone seeing him?

"Nick!" Rebecca yelled. He turned to find her a good six yards behind.

"What's the matter?"

She stood pointing. "Mr. Gibbs's office! Remember?"

He'd sailed right past the jail! He was crazy to think he could do this all alone. Impulsively, he blurted, "We don't need the hat."

Puzzled, Rebecca frowned. "I thought it was a good idea. Wolf's a smart dog. Real smart."

In a low voice, Nick said, "He's in the broken shovel."

Her eyes grew round. "The *soldier*?"

"Shh! Yes, the soldier."

"I want to see him!"

"You can't. It's pitch-black in there. Besides, if you go running to peek, he'll know I told. And he'll figure if I told you, I'm liable to tell anybody."

"But why is he hiding?" Becca protested.

"He's on a military mission and he needs to get back to his base. He's not sure who to trust."

"He can trust me!" she cried.

"But he won't know that!"

"He'll soon see. I want to help, too!"

"You can't, and that's that," Nick insisted.

"Why not?"

"Because he's in my hideout, and that makes him *my* soldier," Nick said impatiently.

"You're not my boss. I'll do what I want!" Rebecca's voice climbed.

She would, too. Thinking fast, Nick said, "You can help me gather together what he needs. I should take it in one trip. If I keep running out there, Mama or Gram'll get curious."

Rebecca jutted out a stubborn chin. "I want to see him."

37

"And you can." Nick softened his tone. "Just before he goes, I'll take you out and tell him that you helped."

"You promise?"

"I promise."

Rebecca gave in with a sigh. "All right. You win. But I still don't understand why he's hiding."

"I told you, he's on a military mission. Top secret," he added for good measure.

"Then he's somebody important?" asked Becca as they started home.

"Real important," said Nick, and he was sure it was true.

Nick tied Wolf to a tree in front of the house. Gram was up. She was at the kitchen table, turning a skein of Red Cross yarn into a scarf for an unknown soldier "over there." Becca and he couldn't very well prepare food or gather supplies with her looking on.

Nick tried to behave as if it were an ordinary afternoon. He went out to play on his scooter. He gave Charlie rides over the sidewalk. By and by, his little brother got sleepy. Mama put him down for a nap, and the afternoon dragged on. The iceman came with a fresh block for the icebox. He awakened Charlie with his jolly booming voice. Having his nap interrupted made Charlie cross. He raised a fuss when Mama left for work.

"Poor lamb!" said Gram. She took him out on the back porch, and sang about Kaiser Bill.

Nick gave Rebecca the nod. She dashed off to get the supplies she'd begun gathering upstairs. Hurriedly, Nick rummaged through the cupboards.

Gram came in with Charlie just as Nick cut a sandwich in half. She frowned at him over the top of her glasses. "I declare, you're your daddy over. Always had to remind that boy to wash his hands. Go on, now, wash them.''

Nick did as he was told. His pulse quickened. He'd carry the sandwich out the door, as if he intended to eat it himself.

But Gram stopped him on the threshold. "Sit down at the table with that. I'll open a jar of peaches and pour you a glass of milk.''

There was nothing to do but sit down at the table. Gram set out leftovers. She was calling Rebecca to come eat when Iris Clark knocked on the back door.

"Come in,'' called Gram. She paused, then exclaimed, "My land, Iris, you're white as a sheet!''

Iris collapsed into a chair. "I've been robbed!''

# Six

———◆———

"Robbed!" cried Becca as Nick fired questions right over her.

"Hush, you two, and let Iris talk." Gram got up from the table and brought Iris a glass of water. "Calm down, now, and start from the beginning."

"It was last evening I saw him." Iris Clark was a little woman with hunched-up shoulders and feet so tiny she bought her shoes in the children's department at Sears & Roebuck. But for all her smallness, she had a voice so large Nick had no doubt but that her words sometimes carried to the next county.

"I glanced out the window, and here came this fellow off the highway," she continued, ringing their ears. "A bum, you could tell by the look of him."

"Vagrant," said Gram, face lined by hard times back in Oklahoma.

"He must have seen me in the window. The next thing I knew, he was coming up the walk. I was switching pocketbooks—that white crocheted purse was soiled. I just can't bear a soiled pocketbook."

"No, of course not." Gram urged her on. "What happened next?"

"The screen was hooked—I'm careful about that. I left both purses on the table and went to the door." Iris's mouth soured at the corners. "I didn't like the looks of him. Oh, he had a polite way of talking. But as he asked for a bite to eat, his gaze was searching my kitchen."

"Did you fix him something?" Becca asked.

"Will you hush, Becca, and let her tell it?" Gram looked at Iris. "Did you fix him something?"

"No, I told him to knock at the back door of the Midway. It just isn't safe for a woman alone to feed bums off the road." Iris angled Gram a sharp glance.

Nick's thoughts skipped to the change missing from E. Z.'s cash drawer. "And this guy robbed you?"

"Not right then. He left. I fixed a bite to eat, listened to the news, then went to bed early. I was in a rush, getting off to work this morning. I didn't miss the white purse. When I got home, I rested a while, then did some chores. It wasn't until I sat down to eat supper that I realized the white purse was gone!"

"But you don't know exactly when it disappeared?"

"That's just what Henry Gibbs asked when I rang him. And, no, I'm afraid I don't."

"How much money did you lose?" asked Gram.

"None. I'd taken my billfold out of the white purse. But there were other things in it—my ration stamps for one. Oh, the shock it gave me to realize my home had been invaded!" Iris shuddered. "The very thought of him stealing into my kitchen while I was sound asleep! I'm staying at my sister's tonight. How else will I get a wink of sleep?"

Nick excused himself from the table and went out on the back step. Becca followed. Nick rolled his eyes and muttered, "Bet she just misplaced the stupid thing."

"If she wasn't so busy minding other people's business, she'd do a better job of minding her own," agreed Becca. She picked at a scab on her knee, then sent him a sidelong glance and dropped her voice to a whisper. "I can't help wondering . . . you don't suppose . . ."

"The soldier?" Nick finished for her. "I'd wonder, too. Except I already asked him about E. Z.'s break-in."

She drew a sharp breath. "You did? What'd he say?"

"Said he never stole anything in his whole life. He's telling the truth, Becca. He's in a fix, that's all. He talks quiet, like Dad."

Thoughtfully, Becca sucked on her bottom lip. "If it was Dad somewhere over *there* hiding out and needing help, I hope God'd nudge somebody to help him. Wouldn't you, Nick?"

"Course," said Nick, though he hadn't until this moment considered God's hand in it. But if it *was* God stirring him to trust the fellow, all the more reason not to disappoint the soldier.

"What're we going to do?" Becca kept her voice low.

"We're going to help, that's what."

Iris stayed a long time. When she left, Gram went upstairs to get ready for work. Charlie trailed after her. Quickly, Nick and Becca made sandwiches for the soldier. They filled a mason jar with warm water from the stove reservoir. Becca got a large enamel basin from beneath the sink.

"He'll need this to soak his ankle."

Nick nodded. The space of time between when Gram left for work and Mama came home was when he would go. He'd have ten minutes to spend with the soldier. Fifteen, if Mama dawdled.

Nick followed Becca into the living room. He turned on the radio and waited for it to warm up. Before Dad went overseas *The Green Hornet* had been Nick's favorite program. Now he listened first for war news.

Gram Kelsey came down the stairs at the sound of the radio crackling. It was almost time for her to go. But she dallied a moment, hands tightly clenched as the newscaster announced that American troops were scrambling to cut off the German's last rail escape route out of Cherbourg.

"Thrash those Nazis till they throw down their guns and run home, tails tucked," said Gram in a low fierce voice. She grabbed up her purse and started out the door.

Nick walked with her to the corner beneath a starlit sky. "We're winning, aren't we?" he ventured.

"I pray to God we are," she said fervently. "Bless our brave boys."

"A fella should help the soldiers every chance he gets, shouldn't he, Gram?"

"Absolutely," said Gram. "Sacrifice the comforts, gladly. The necessities, too, when it comes to that. It's the least we can do."

"That's what I thought," murmured Nick.

Gram indicated Miss Clark's home in passing and said in a lighter tone, "Iris went to her sister's home, sure enough. Her house is dark."

"Do you think the vagrant really broke in and stole her purse?" Nick asked.

43

"With the eyes and ears on that woman?" Gram's mouth twitched. "It's a stretch of the imagination. But then, stranger things have happened. This here's far enough," she said when they reached the railroad tracks. "You go on home now."

Nick needed no further urging.

Becca was wrapping a bottle of iodine in a rag. "He might need this for his cuts."

Nick started out the kitchen door carrying the basin and all it contained. Wolf, still tied around front, whined. The whine turned to a growl. Nick looked toward the barn.

It was as if the vagrant stepped out of the star-studded sky into Gram's Victory garden. Nick dropped the basin on the steps and backed hastily into the kitchen.

Dressed in an oversized coat, the man made a ragged shadow beneath the night sky. A weather-stained slouch hat hid his face. His shoulders were stooped. He leaned on a stick and moved at an awkward shuffle.

"What's wrong?" asked Becca.

Wordlessly, Nick pointed.

Becca sucked in her breath. "He must be the one Iris saw! I don't like him. Lock the door, quick."

Nick locked the door. He turned out the kitchen light and moved cautiously to the window. The vagrant stooped over and pulled a vegetable from the garden.

Rebecca lifted Charlie into her arms and held him close. "It's okay, Charlie. The bad man can't get you."

"You're being plain silly! He's hungry, that's all." Nick didn't let on that his own heart was pounding.

The man devoured whatever it was he'd pulled, then pulled another.

Wolf's growls exploded into a volley of deep, angry barks.

Fresh urgency marked the man's movements. He nearly toppled over in his haste. He uprooted entire green bean plants and stuffed them inside his jacket.

Becca gasped. "Look what he's doing! There won't be any left to can!"

His father would never allow a stranger to destroy Gram's garden! Nick sprang across the kitchen.

"Where are you going?" cried Becca.

"To let Wolf go."

"He'll tear him to pieces!"

Nick envisioned Wolf leaping upon the man, sinking his teeth in deep. What if Wolf *did* tear him to pieces?

"Henry Gibbs'll shoot him," Becca warned. "He will, Nick! He shot that old dog that bit the station manager. Don't let him go! Wait until Mama gets here."

A second scene flashed through Nick's mind—Mama, starting down those stairs alone. He'd couldn't let his father down again. "I'll tie him around back. That'll scare him off. Run upstairs and watch for Mama. You can see better from the bedroom windows."

Nick clamored down the stairs and flew across the musty basement. He freed the bolt on the cellar door and let himself out. Wolf was tied several yards away. Nick loosed the rope from the tree.

The dog lunged. The rope seared Nick's hands. "Heel, Wolf! Heel!" he shouted.

The dog strained forward on powerful limbs. The ruff of hair on his neck stood up. His barking grew more frenzied.

"Down! Stop! Down!" panted Nick, hanging on for dear life. But his attempts to stop the dog were futile. Wolf dragged him around the house and on toward the garden.

45

The vagrant was trying his best to flee. But he was heavily built and already winded. "Hang onto that dog, lad! Don't turn him loose!" he wheezed.

"Run, mister! I can't hold him much longer." Nick's chest heaved. His hands throbbed from his vain effort to control Wolf. A yard ahead was the water pump. If only he could ... "Down, Wolf! Down!" He jerked hard on the rope.

Wolf hesitated and looked back at him. It was the split second Nick needed. He hitched the rope around the pump pipe and prayed it would hold. He flew to the cellar, bolted the door behind him and tore across the dark basement to the kitchen stairs. Above, the kitchen door yawned open. Nick's heart stopped. His whole body froze.

At the top of the stairs a hulking shape blocked out the light!

The shriek was out of Nick's mouth before he could stop it.

"Nick, what's got into you? And that dog! Lord have mercy!"

It was Mama! Before his very eyes, the shape seemed to shrink and lose its dark threatening demeanor. Weak with relief, Nick hung on to the rail as he climbed the stairs. Becca spilled the whole story before he ever made it to the top.

Mama walked out on the porch, the children at her heels. She looked toward the garden. There was no one to be seen. "He must have moved on."

She hooked the screen door, then closed and locked the inside door as well. She stooped to pick up Charlie, then settled her gaze on Nick. "You're a mite peaked."

Nick tried to deny that he was frightened. But his

voice betrayed him. "I c-couldn't let him t-tear up Gram's garden."

"I don't imagine he meant any harm. He must have been very hungry."

"I bet it was the same man who asked Miss Clark for food yesterday," said Becca. She went on to relay their neighbor's story. But before she got to the part about the missing pocketbook, Mama drew in a sharp breath.

"Nick!" she exclaimed. "What's happened to your hands?"

Her alarm made the pain worse. Nick turned his palms up, exposing red, rope-burned flesh. Mama set a protesting Charlie in a chair. She reached under the sink for the basin.

"Now where's that gotten off to?"

As she searched for the basin Nick had left out on the porch, Becca told how valiantly Nick had clung to Wolf's rope. Becca's admiring tone soothed Nick's ears. But it didn't help his hands at all. Mama gave up looking for the basin. She led him to the sink and pumped a little water over his hands.

"Just look at you. Turning Wolf loose, indeed! Why, that dog would have torn that man limb from limb! Gram's right, you know. That imagination of yours is going to get you in trouble."

"Twubble," echoed Charlie solemnly.

Nick laughed and Becca joined in. Mama chuckled too and said more gently, "Hold still, Nick. Becca, get the salve."

Salve made Nick think of iodine. Iodine reminded him of the soldier. The soldier must be very hungry by now. What was he to do? Wait until Mama went to bed? Slip out in the night?

An image of the vagrant flashed before his eyes. A tremor traveled the length of his body.

Misunderstanding, Mama paused in tending his hands. "Sorry, Nickie. I'm being as easy as I can."

# Seven

Nick was ready for bed when he remembered Wolf. The dog was still tied to the pump around back. He'd been pretty excited over the vagrant. What if he caught the soldier's scent and started barking again?

While Mama was busy getting Charlie ready for bed, Nick slipped downstairs and out the door. It made his skin prickle to think of the raggedy vagrant. But once he reached Wolf he felt safe. He buried his face in the dog's neck.

"Good dog. You'll keep watch won't you? Come around front. I'll get you fresh water."

Nick filled the dish and gave the dog a hug before returning to his room. Mama was finishing prayers with Becca and Charlie.

"And please bring Daddy home soon," she said.

Charlie reached for the picture on the table. "Cha-wee's da-da?"

"Yes, Charlie's da-da." Mama patted the bed for Nick to come jump in, saying to Charlie, "Do you want to hear a story about Daddy?"

Becca leaned into Mama, urging, "Tell a long one."

Mama gathered them all close and began, "Grandpa Kelsey farmed back in Oklahoma, you know, and Gram took in laundry just to make ends meet. She had a washhouse in the backyard. Every morning after breakfast, she would go out there to wash. Sometimes, she had so much laundry to do, she didn't even take time to clear away breakfast dishes. It was a morning like that she'd asked Grandpa to keep an eye on the baby."

"That'd be Daddy," Becca interrupted.

"Yes, Daddy. He was just a year old, not even as big as you, Charlie. Grandpa said sure, he'd watch the baby. His wooden leg was troubling him, and he was resting while he read the paper."

"Is this where Daddy pulled the butter dish off the breakfast table?" asked Becca.

"Hush, and let Mama tell it," complained Nick.

"That's what he did, just like Becca said. Quiet as a mouse, Daddy played in that butter, making pat-a-cakes." Mama paused to pat-a-cake Charlie's hands together. "Butter'd set out awhile, so it was nice and soft. Daddy smeared it on his clothes and through his curls and over his little cheeks. He rubbed it on the table legs, over the chair seats, and on Gram's kitchen floor."

"Little stinker!" said Becca, giggling.

Nick knew it was for Charlie Mama told these stories. Charlie was too young to remember their father. The story made Nick smile all the same.

"Gram came in to find him spreading that butter from one end of her kitchen to the other!" Mama was saying. "For years after that, she called Daddy her little butter boy."

"Buttah boy!" Charlie echoed their laughter. He

smudged the picture glass with a damp finger. "Da-da, Da-da."

At the familiar name, Nick felt a melting inside and wrenching of heart. So much had happened since he'd heard the porch boards creak the previous night. He thought of the soldier hiding out in the barn. Keeping his secret, searching for a way to care for him was a heavy load. His hands stung and he was weary through and through.

Seeing the tears in his eyes, Mama hugged him close. "We can only pray this war'll be over soon. Then Daddy will come home to stay." She kissed his forehead, adding, "Maybe there'll be a letter tomorrow."

Her voice was so gentle, so understanding, Nick was tempted to tell her about the soldier. She could go out with him to care for the fellow. But he'd already broken his promise to the soldier once by telling Becca. And grown-ups, once a secret was told, had a way of taking over.

"Mama?" he asked. "Did the Army ever call Henry Gibbs back?"

"He hadn't heard a word when I left." Mama brushed his hair back from his forehead. "Would you stop worrying over the fellow? I'm sure he's safely back wherever he was headed."

Nick lay waiting for the house to grow still. His eyes were heavy. But he didn't dare close them. All day, the soldier had waited. He couldn't fail him. Questions circled in his mind. What was his name? Where was he from? What was his military mission? Did the safety of the country hinge on his success or failure?

The lights of passing vehicles followed the familiar

path through Nick's room. His thoughts drifted, harmonizing with the sounds from the hard road. He tried to calm himself, thinking, as he often did, of all the people who passed his house—people from all over the country, old people and young ones, truck drivers and school-teachers and factory workers, soldiers and civilians, singers and dancers and everyday people. How strange to think they came so close and yet never met.

Mama said that when Dad came home, maybe they'd take a trip on 66. Follow it clear out to California. He'd pass the homes of children not so different from him.

Yes, Route 66 was a wonder. A wrinkle across the continent, weaving its way through the lives of so many. Nick yawned. His eyes drifted shut. The melody of the hard road faded away, and he slept.

It was a nagging urgency that awakened him. He lay a moment, clearing the dreams from his head. The soldier! How long had he slept? He slid out of bed and tiptoed to the window. A slice of moon shone from a slate-black sky.

Nick pulled on his trousers. At the top of the landing, he listened hard. No one was stirring. He felt his way down the stairs and to the kitchen where he lobbed off a chunk of cheese and stuffed it in his pocket.

The metallic click of the lock turning echoed off the walls. Nick's heartbeat quickened. He listened for Mama's light step overhead. But all was still.

He slipped out the door onto the porch. The bottom step was empty. His heart dropped. The basin and all the supplies were gone! He fell to his knees to explore the dew-slickened grass.

What had happened to the sandwiches? The water? The other supplies? Had Mama found them? No, she would have said something. The vagrant in the garden? Had he taken them? And if so, where was he now? Nick's pulse quickened, his heart thumping so hard it hurt. The trees and bushes swayed in the breeze. Their shadowy shapes seemed to come to life.

He closed his eyes and drew in a deep, steadying breath. What was he to do? He had nothing to take the soldier. Wolf whined in the night, sending tiny prickles down Nick's nerve endings. Clouds scudded across the moon. He picked his way along to the tree where the dog was tied.

"Here, boy," he whispered and gave him the cheese. "You hush now. Not a sound."

If the vagrant had taken the supplies, why hadn't Wolf barked? Had he been sleeping? Well, he was wide awake now. Wouldn't he be barking if the man were close by?

Feeling somewhat braver, Nick circled back the way he'd come. He could not go in until he'd talked to the soldier. Explained why he'd failed him. He sped across the damp, fragrant meadow and knocked at the door of the broken shovel.

"Hey, mister. It's me, Nick."

His keen ears picked up the sound of rustling straw. A voice, gravelly with sleep called back to him: "Shouldn't you be in bed?"

"Something happened earlier, and I couldn't come." Hesitantly, Nick opened the door to the granary. It was too dark to see the soldier. Though it was *his* secret place, he was hesitant at this late, dark hour to go in. From the open door, he told about the vagrant. He finished with the unhappy news that the supplies he'd prepared had disappeared.

"I got them," said the soldier. "I was watching through a knothole when you dropped them on the step."

"You saw the man, then?"

"Yes, I saw him," he said.

The hair rose on the back of Nick's neck. "Did you see where he went?"

"He headed north up the highway."

"Toward Midway Truck Stop?"

"As far as I could tell."

Nick let go a sigh of relief. "You got the sandwiches, then? And the iodine for your cuts?"

"I got it all."

"How's your ankle?"

"Still pretty tender."

"I'll try to bring you something to eat in the morning," Nick said.

"You best get back now, before you're missed."

But Nick was wide awake now. He knew it would be a while before he could sleep again. Soundlessly, he crept into his father's pickup truck. Though the scent of his father's cigars had long since faded, he felt closer to him here than anywhere else on the place. In his mind was a picture of his father behind the wheel. Strong brown hand on the shift knob, scarred boots on the pedals, his hat cocked back. Nick sat thinking of him and casting an occasional glance toward the granary door.

The knothole the soldier had mentioned—he knew very well its exact location. More than once, he'd kept watch at that knothole. He hadn't wanted Mama to slip out to the barn and catch him and his friend Billy with the lantern burning.

Nick leaned forward. He rested his head against his arms. He was so tired, his thoughts came in disjointed flashes. He recalled the sensation he'd felt earlier when he'd been weeding Gram's garden—it must have been the soldier watching him! Had he watched the house all day? Had he seen him hoeing the garden, Becca hanging the wash? Why, he may have even overheard their conversation as they'd played in the truck.

If so, he'd known even before Nick jumped into the broken shovel that they were eager to help. Tired though he was, Nick took pride in the knowledge that he and Becca had helped the man. In so doing, they were helping their country, too.

# Eight

Mama awakened Nick the next morning. It was Saturday and she didn't have to go to work until after lunch. But she was dressed to go out.

"I've got a bit of shopping to do. Becca's coming with me." She clipped on earrings that matched her Victory pin. "Your breakfast is on the table. You'll have to watch Charlie."

"Is Gram sleeping?"

"Yes. She's had another busy night. Doc Carbury's house was broken into. Doc heard glass shatter and went to investigate. The intruder heard him coming and ran. Doc called Henry right away."

Nick was suddenly wide awake. "Did Mr. Gibbs catch him?"

"Not at Doc's house. But he's holding a man for questioning." Mama smoothed her dress, adding, "A vagrant. He picked him up a few miles out of town."

"Do you think it's the fellow who tramped through Gram's garden?"

"Could be. According to Gram, Henry's questioning

him about the money missing from E. Z.'s cash drawer, too.''

The soldier'd been upset when he'd learned of the first break-in. It made him even more reluctant to seek help, lest he be suspected on the grounds he was a stranger and in need. But if Constable Gibbs had picked up the vagrant, then his soldier was in the clear, wasn't he? *Wasn't he?* Course he was. Ashamed of a fleeting ''what if,'' Nick warded it off and trailed her down the stairs.

''What about the number in the soldier's hat? Did the Army call Constable Gibbs back?''

''Gram didn't mention it.'' Mama pinned on her hat, took one last sip of her coffee, and grimaced. ''Roosevelt coffee,'' wagered Nick. That's what she called it when she used the grounds twice, another sacrifice for the war.

Mama'd left a plate of bacon, scrambled eggs, and toasted bread warming on the stove. Nick was hungry. But he knew he should give it to the soldier. Taking Charlie with him, he dressed quickly, then returned to the kitchen for the plate.

''Let's go, Charlie. Push the screen open for me, that's a time.''

Charlie let the screen door slam and backed down the steps after Nick. But he stopped short at the grass and held up his arms to be carried.

''I've got my hands full. You can walk.''

Charlie gingerly touched one foot to the damp grass and pulled back. He poked out his bottom lip and lifted reproachful eyes.

''Oh, all right!'' Caving in, Nick left the glass of milk and lugged Charlie on one hip. Just yards from the barn, a piece of bacon slid off the plate. He set

57

Charlie down, picked up the bacon, and blew off the dandelion fluff.

"Come on, Charlie. Walk!" he coaxed.

*"Whah-ah-ah,"* whined Charlie, sounding just like Dad's truck when it wouldn't turn over.

"All right, then. Just stay where you are if you're gonna be stubborn."

Charlie whimpered and called after him, "Nickie, cahwee, Nickie, cahwee!"

Nick hardened his heart and marched on to the barn alone.

"Mister? I brought you some breakfast."

"Anyone see you?"

"Just my little brother, and he's a baby."

The door squeaked open. The hand that reached for the plate was large, the fingers stained with tobacco. "Looks good."

Nick's stomach rumbled in agreement. "There's a glass of milk, too. I'll run get it."

"No need. This'll do. Thanks, son."

Nick wanted to stay longer. He had yet to see the man's face. And there were so many questions to ask. He hadn't told him the news about the vagrant, either. He stood a moment, drawn to the man by his soldier status, yet intimidated, too, and faintly uncomfortable. As he searched for words, Charlie's whimpers grew to a soulful wail. Wolf barked in sympathy. Between the two of them, they were sure to awaken Gram. Nick turned away, saying, "I'll try to come back this evening."

But he knew it wouldn't be easy. It was Saturday. Mama had to work from one until nine. And come evening, Gram would be taking him and Becca and Charlie to see Annie and the Wranglers perform. It was a free

58

music show. Midway Truck Stop sponsored it every Saturday night of the summer. Gram usually stayed until time for her shift. Then they walked with her to the telephone office. Mama accompanied them home. How was he to fit a trip to the barn into that?

Nick gave his little brother a piggyback ride to the house. He poured the glass of milk over cold cereal and shared it with Charlie. They played with building blocks until Becca came racing in. She dropped her parcels on the table and fell into a chair, dark curls clinging damply to her brow.

"I ran all the way. Mr. Gibbs got a return call from Fort Leonard Wood. They don't have anyone there with identification numbers to match those in the hat."

That really wasn't so surprising, reasoned Nick. The soldier was on a secret military mission. He wasn't necessarily *from* Fort Leonard Wood. He'd never said what his home base was.

Becca tossed a furtive glance over her shoulder, just to make certain Mama hadn't caught up yet. She dropped her voice to a whisper. "How'd you manage last night? Did you get the supplies to him?"

"Yes, and some breakfast this morning."

"Did you find out who he is?"

"There's been no time to talk," Nick said, seized again by a vague uneasiness, yet unable to express it.

"Mr. Gibbs hasn't learned anything, either. Except that an initial and four digits of an identification number is next to impossible to trace."

Becca clammed up as Mama came in carrying her wicker shopping basket, her pocketbook, and the mail. She tore into an envelope, smiling so broadly, Nick's heart bumped.

"Is that from Dad?" he cried.

"Aunt Susan," said Becca knowingly.

Nick watched Mama's gaze race across a lined page. Both sides were filled with a familiar backward scrawl. He recovered from his initial disappointment enough to ask, "What's she have to say?"

Mama chuckled and glanced up from the letter. "You know those burros that wander the streets in that town where Susan and Russell settled after his medical discharge? Well, Kathleen was in her high chair near an open window when one of those critters stuck his head through and ate a biscuit right off her tray!"

"A donkey ate the baby's biscuit?" Becca giggled. "Did it scare her?"

Mama wagged her head and read aloud: " 'Not quite two, and a regular little desert rat already. She cries after Russell every time he puts on his prospecting hat and heads out to explore. But Russell's nerves are still fragile and he won't take her unless I go along. These desert mountains are so desolate and dry, it makes Oklahoma look like an oasis. I'd trade every last cactus for one big old oak tree.' "

"Sounds like the baby loves Arizona a lot better'n Aunt Susan," said Becca.

"Suker always did go on about trees," said Mama. "Course Russell's desert born. He may not understand yet how towering green trees feed Suker's soul."

"Suker" was Aunt Susan's childhood nickname. Sometimes Mama still called her that. Gram Sophie and Grandpa Dave, and Jeremiah too. They all adored Aunt Susan, even if she wasn't a blood relative.

"Does she say anything about Uncle Razz?" asked Becca.

"He isn't really our uncle," said Nick, for he hadn't forgotten how cool Dad had been toward Razz at Aunt Susan's wedding, the only time Nick'd ever met Razz. He didn't want to risk being disloyal.

Deaf ear to both of them, Mama read to herself a bit further, then exclaimed in surprise, "My stars, Razz has married an English girl!"

"You talking about Razz Tucker?" Gram padded into the kitchen in her warm robe and slippers and said with a sniff, "Doubt he could find an American girl willing to take a chance on him."

"Says here she's a rector's daughter."

"My, is *she* in for a rude awakening!"

"Leota!" said Mama. But repressed laughter contradicted the censure in her tone.

"Can't help it. That boy and I got off on the wrong foot. I never did get over it entirely," admitted Gram.

"What's a rector?" asked Becca.

"A minister. That's what they call them in England," said Mama. "Apparently, Razz met the girl while recovering from a bullet wound in a London hospital."

"A Nazi shot Uncle Razz?" cried Becca. Nick recalled then that Becca had been quite taken with Aunt Susan's brother.

"Susan says he's doing fine now and is back at the front again," said Mama. "No time even for a honeymoon."

"Well, I'm sorry he got shot," said Gram grudgingly. "Don't like to hear of any of our boys being injured. But he *did* cause Rob trouble that time. That vagrant being jailed reminded me, I guess."

Nick's ears tingled. "What kind of trouble, Gram?"

"You've never heard how your daddy spent a night in jail, thanks to Razz Tucker?" asked Gram.

"Daddy? In jail?" squealed Becca. "How come?"

"A little misunderstanding over a Christmas tree," said Mama, laugh lines framing her eyes.

"Misunderstanding, my foot!" exclaimed Gram. "Razz Tucker and two other boys chopped a cedar down in the cemetery back home and dragged it into church for a Christmas tree. Your mama's neighbor, Miss Tims, called the law on them. What'd Razz do but claim my Rob had a part in it, too. There we were, Christmas around the corner, our youngest in jail, the Depression upon us, and no money to bail him out!"

Gram's eyes snapped at the very thought. But Mama tossed her head and laughed out loud. "Be fair now and tell the rest of it. Razz owned up to the truth, finally," she said, when Gram seemed reluctant. "It turned out to be a nice Christmas after all."

"What happened to Uncle Razz?" asked Becca. "Did he stay in jail for Christmas?"

Mama wagged her head. "Thanks to Miss Tims who put him there, Razz got out long enough to enjoy a party at our house. The party was Suker and little Jere's Christmas surprise. They were something, weren't they, inviting all those people without telling Mama? Tickles me even now to think of it."

It was good to hear Mama laugh. For a while, as she shared stories of hard but memorable times, the war seemed far away. But too soon, the telling was over. Lunch, too, and Mama set off to work.

Iris Clark phoned Gram late in the afternoon to say she'd identified the man at the jail as the same vagrant who'd come to her door. Positively, no doubt about it. Much to her indignation, he denied taking her purse. He denied breaking into E. Z.'s shop and Dr. Carbury's home, too. But according to Gram, Iris didn't for a moment believe him.

Was it for sure the fellow who'd invaded Gram's garden? Nick wanted to see for himself, for Dad always said you could read a lot in a man's face if you looked closely. Course Gram wouldn't cooperate.

"You leave that man be," she warned. "I won't have the whole town talking about us begrudging a vagrant a few green beans."

Gram wasn't usually so short with him. But she hadn't gotten enough sleep. Her head ached. And most likely, she was counting the days since they'd had a letter from Dad. Six, now. Six days since his last letter. Eleven days since the Normandy invasion first began. Nick knew well enough. He also knew that if Gram didn't get to feeling better, they wouldn't be going to see Annie and the Wranglers that evening. It was an event he always enjoyed, and he was looking forward to it even more than usual as a distraction from his worries. Becca didn't want to miss the show either, so they occupied Charlie and helped Gram all they could. Sure enough, their efforts paid off.

"Get the washtub," said Gram right after supper. "You kids'll have to clean up if we're going."

Spirits lifting, Nick drew water from the stove reservoir and mixed it with cool water to get just the right temperature. Gram bathed Charlie in the washtub while he and Becca washed and wiped the dishes dry. By the time he and Rebecca had bathed, and they'd gotten to Midway, Annie and the Wranglers were tuning up.

The parking lot was crowded with cars and trucks and people. A hay wagon was the stage. It was parked in the grassy field at the edge of the parking lot. Annie and her Wrangler band were dressed in boots and hats and fancy fringed clothes. The gathering crowd swayed to the music as Annie wailed the opening song.

Rebecca and Nick ran to spread their blanket on the grass. Gram waved and called a greeting to Iris Clark: "If I'd known you were coming, we could have all walked over together."

"It's only because Henry caught that bum that I'm here. Otherwise, I couldn't have gone home to a dark house," said Iris in her clamorous voice.

Nick leaned across Becca to ask, "Did you talk to the man in jail?"

Iris sniffed. "Certainly not! One look at his shifty eyes was enough. Not to mention his limp."

"The man in the garden was stowed up too," said Nick.

Iris nodded knowingly. "The fellow has a stiff knee, according to Henry."

"A stiff knee? You mean it won't bend? I'd like to see that," said Becca.

"You've got the best show in town right before your eyes. I don't want to hear another word about that vagrant." Gram folded her sturdy hands around Charlie's. She helped him clap to the music.

Nick clapped too, and laughed at Annie's sharp wit. For the first time all day, he wasn't thinking of the soldier at all until a military convoy pulled off Route 66. The parking lot was full. They had to park along the side streets across from Midway.

Soldiers trooped into the truck stop for a late dinner.

Most of them came back out to watch the show while they ate. People squeezed together and made room. Charlie got all big eyed. He pointed to the nearest fellow in a uniform, and asked repeatedly, "Da-da? Da-da?"

"No, Charlie. It's not your daddy," Gram told him time and again.

At intermission, Nick nudged Becca and said in a low voice, "I'm going to run home and take care of you know who."

Becca nodded and whispered, "The sandwiches are all ready. They're wrapped in a dishcloth under the porch steps."

Nick shot Gram a quick glance. She was engaged in conversation with Iris. He edged off the blanket. "If Gram misses me, tell her I've gone to get an ice cream."

Becca warned, "Hurry, or she'll get suspicious."

Nick noticed as he crossed the highway that the windows of E. Z.'s Mechanic Shop were dark. Doc Carbury's house looked deserted, too. Most everyone in town was at the show. To the west, a lavender sky blended heaven with earth.

Nick heard Wolf barking and quickened his steps. The dog was no doubt disturbed by the flood of military vehicles. He'd have to shut him up before returning to the show or the neighbors, upon arriving home from the show, would be sure to complain.

But first things first. The soldier had waited all day, and Nick's questions had waited too. Eager to lay niggling doubts to rest, Nick circled to the back of the house. All at once, his heart stood still. Before his very eyes, a dark shape separated itself from deep shadow. He gasped as it bounded down the back steps toward him.

# Nine

&#x2014;&#x25C6;&#x2014;

Nick let out a squeal as a hand closed over his shoulder and turned him around.

"Easy there. I didn't mean to frighten you."

It was a soldier peering down at him. A captain, judging by the bars on his shirt. Short in stature, clean-shaven, and neat, there was nothing threatening in his demeanor. Nick stopped struggling. Flushing, he squeaked a timid, "Sir?"

"I'm Captain Anderson. Do you know where I can find the owner of this pasture?"

"That'd be us. My mother, I mean," Nick amended.

"You live here?" the captain asked.

"Yes, sir."

"No one answered the door."

"Mama's at work. I just came from the show at Midway," Nick explained.

"I see. Where does your mother work?"

"The telephone office. Are you with the convoy?" Nick asked.

Captain Anderson nodded.

"You can use the pasture if you want to."

"I was hoping we might. But I need to speak to your mother about it."

"She won't care. Soldiers pass by all the time. You won't be the first to camp here," Nick said.

"Still, I'd like to ask her permission. Would it be a problem if I contacted her at work?" asked the captain.

"No. Tell her I sent you. I'm Nick. Nick Kelsey," he added.

Captain Anderson shook his hand. "It's nice meeting you, Nick. Is the telephone office far from here?"

"Just a few blocks." Nick pointed toward the center of town and gave the man directions. He accompanied him to the front yard and out to the waiting jeep. Captain Anderson climbed in, tipped his hat, and thanked Nick for his trouble.

Wolf snarled and flung himself to the end of the rope in a vain effort to reach the departing jeep. The taillights winked in the dusk as the vehicle rattled down the street and over the railroad tracks. Nick stroked Wolf's ruffled fur and tried to calm him.

Whenever soldiers camped in the pasture, Mama put Wolf in the basement. There was a key hidden behind the down spout at the back of the house. Nick unlocked the door and took Wolf down. He returned the key to its hiding place. How long had he been gone? Gram would be wondering about him. And he hadn't yet taken the sandwiches to the soldier.

The soldier! He had to tell him the troops would be bivouacking in the pasture. Maybe Captain Anderson could take the man to where he needed to go. It could be the perfect solution. Nick was surprised by the weight lifting from his shoulders at the thought of a solution to this soldier problem. But just as he angled for the barn, a familiar voice stopped him.

"So *here* you are!"

Gram's glasses rode low on her nose as she scowled at him in the gathering darkness. Rebecca was a few yards behind. She shifted Charlie from one hip to the other. "See, Gram, I *told* you he didn't go to the jail."

"Well, what was I to think? He's been itching all day to have a look at the vagrant." Gram defended her suspicion. She gave her glasses a nudge and demanded, "What's got into you, Nick? Why'd you leave the show without telling me?"

"The soldiers are going to camp in the pasture," said Nick.

"Oh, boy!" Becca clapped in anticipation, for soldiers, homesick for their own children or younger siblings, generally made a fuss over the children. Becca loved the attention.

"A Captain Anderson just asked permission," Nick went on. "I told him it'd be all right, but he wanted to ask Mama. So I sent him to the telephone office."

Gram scratched her head and tried to puzzle it out. "But how did this fellow pick you out of . . . oh, never mind!" She gave up. "Let's go inside."

"Aren't we going back to Midway? The show isn't over," Becca objected.

"It is for us," said Gram. "My head is throbbing. I've got to have a cup of tea and a little rest before I go to work."

"If you want to lie down, I'll bring your tea up to you," Nick offered, as Gram unlocked the door.

68

Gram softened some. "Thank you. That would be nice."

"Would you like some crackers and butter, too?" Nick asked.

"I believe I would, if it's not too much trouble." Gram tramped through the dark living room.

Nick heard her climb the stairs. He stirred the fire to life and put on water to boil. Becca got crackers and a dish of softened butter from the cupboard.

"Me-me," Charlie stretched out a hand.

Nick gave him a buttered cracker. He nudged Becca. "I've got to tell the soldier what's happening. Maybe these guys can help him."

"Go on, then. I'll take Gram's tea," Becca said.

Nick got the sandwiches from beneath the porch. He raced out to the barn. He knocked on the door of the broken shovel. "Mister?"

There was no answer. He knocked again, then pushed the door open a crack. It was too dark to see, but the odors were the same. He felt certain the soldier was there. Hesitantly, he said, "Mister? You all right?"

Still no answer. Was he sick? Had he passed out? Feeling uneasy, Nick climbed up on the stack of boards outside the door and poked his head in. "Mister?"

Failing to get a response, he jumped over the threshold into the granary. His feet no more than hit the floor when two strong hands grabbed him in the darkness. "Did you give me away, boy?" a low voice rumbled.

"No! Course not!" Nick yelped, startled by the hardness of his tone.

"I saw you talking to that officer and pointing out this way. Gone for the constable, has he?"

Nick tried to wrench free. "You've got it all wrong.

69

That's Captain Anderson. He's with a convoy off the highway. He went uptown to ask my mother permission to camp in the pasture.''

Vicelike fingers tightened around Nick's upper arms. ''This pasture?''

Nick nodded.

''Just when I thought it couldn't get any worse!'' muttered the soldier. He let go of Nick and hit the wall with a fist, making Nick jump. ''Nothing's gone right. Half starved. This hot dusty barn. Ankle's giving me fits. And now soldiers setting up camp!''

Nick lifted a bewildered gaze to the soldier's face, hoping he was wrong about the awful doubts taking shape in his mind. ''I brought you sandwiches,'' he said in a small voice.

''Hush, would you, and let me think!''

It was too dark to make out his features. But a forelock of hair fell across the fellow's forehead as he peered out the knothole and back again. An icy chill shot through Nick. His hair! It wasn't cut military style. He didn't act like a soldier, either. Thankless, self-pitying, grabbing him so rough. But if he wasn't a soldier, who was he? Nick shivered in the warm fetid air.

''I've got to get away from here,'' the man muttered out loud. ''How am I going to get away? Think! I've gotta think!''

The room was closing in on Nick. The door was the only avenue of escape. But he didn't dare lunge for it. The man was big and strong, despite his injuries. Heeding an inner warning, he tried to mask his exploding mistrust and fear. ''Here's the sandwiches, if you're hungry.''

The man stared at him intently, then abruptly reached

70

for the sandwiches. Nick let them fall to the granary floor. "Oops. Sorry."

As the man stooped to retrieve them, Nick leaped toward the door. He was scrambling over and out when the man caught him by the back of the shirt and pushed him into a corner.

"You sit right there, sonny! Don't you move!" he hissed, the quiet politeness of yesterday gone from his voice.

Nick shrank against the boards, heart pounding. How could he have thought this man was kind and decent like his father? How had he been so easily deceived? Something was bunched up in the straw beneath him. But the discomfort of a lump prodding his backside was nothing compared to the fingers of fear clawing at his chest, threatening to choke off the air to his lungs as the man towered over him, prodding the air with a finger.

"No more funny business," he warned. "I'm in a bad way and in no mood to play games. Understand?"

The man glared at Nick until he nodded acquiescence, then spared a quick glance out the knothole again. As he looked away, Nick shifted and with one hand explored the straw beneath his bottom. The lump had a familiar feel to it: fabric, woven, like the pot holders he'd made on the loom Gram had bought him last Christmas only bigger, thicker, as if it were doubled. A pocketbook! Iris Clark's crocheted pocketbook! This man *had* stolen it! The vagrant had been falsely blamed! Nick drew a swift breath as the man reached down and yanked him to his feet.

"Here's what you're gonna do. You're gonna go in the house. You're gonna get me the key to that truck. And you're gonna bring it back to me."

71

"It doesn't run."

"Don't you lie to me, boy! I heard you and your sister out there playing. It runs all right, and you're gonna get me the key. Is that clear?" The man shook him so hard, a sob escaped.

Instinctively, Nick lashed back, kicking the man's wounded ankle.

The man yelled in pain and hobbled on one foot. Taking advantage of the fellow's unsteady balance, Nick shoved him hard. He fell to the floor. A howl followed Nick out of the granary. He left the barn behind and was halfway across the meadow when he heard the man coming after him. Stumbling in panic, he fell in the dewy grass, picked himself up, and ran on.

The back porch was just ahead. The man could not catch him. He had only to lock the door. Yell for Gram. Ring the telephone office. Mama'd summon Henry Gibbs. They'd be safe.

Nick burst through the back door, hollering, "Gram! Gram!" Inexplicably, his feet flew out from beneath him. He slid across the floor and tangled himself up in the legs of a kitchen chair.

Charlie, hunkered beneath the table, blinked at him. He pressed his butter-coated hands to his oily cheeks and babbled proudly, "Buttah, buttah, buttah boy."

Becca raced into the kitchen. She looked in astonishment from a butter-coated Charlie to Nick, and stopped just short of laughter.

"Lock the door!" Nick screamed at her. "Lock the door! Ring Henry Gibbs!"

The urgency in his voice washed the color from Becca's face. Stunned, she stood motionless. Nick scram-

72

bled to his feet and turned the lock himself just as the knob rattled from the outside.

Becca cried, "What is it? Who is it, Nick?"

"He's a burglar. He stole Miss Clark's purse!" Nick sped to the phone box on the wall, turned the crank furiously, leaned into the mouthpiece and hollered, "Mama! Mama! Send Mr. Gibbs quick!"

At the same moment, the door burst open. It was the man Nick had cared for with such patriotic concern. He held the key from the downspout in one hand. "Hang it up!" he warned in a voice hard as steel.

Had Mama heard from her place at the switchboard? Had she opened the key and plugged it in in time to open the line and hear his plea?

# Ten

———◆———

"**I** said, hang it up!"
No soldier at all, rather, a dangerous intruder in a dirty, ill-fitting uniform, the man shifted his weight to favor his injured ankle, watching from glittering eyes as Nick did his bidding. "That's better. Now get me that truck key."

"I'm not sure where Mama keeps it," Nick fibbed.

"Don't lie to me! You get it and fast!" The intruder lunged toward Becca and scooped her in with one arm. "Or else."

"Do it, Nick!" whimpered Becca, ashen faced.

Charlie crawled from beneath the table and ogled the uniformed stranger as Nick picked his way across the buttered floor. Wolf sprang at the door leading from the basement into the kitchen. He clawed and barked ferociously at the solid wood that barred his entry. At the same moment, Gram clattered down from upstairs, calling, "What's all the ruckus?"

"He's a burglar, Gram!" Nick blurted as she swept into the kitchen.

"Yes, and if it weren't for my ankle and a string of rotten luck, I'd have acquired enough cash to be long gone by now. The key, boy!"

Taking it in at a glance, Gram caught Nick by the arm and held him back. "Let my granddaughter go, then you can have the key. Charlie, Becca, come to Gram."

"The key first!" said the stranger. Emboldened by Gram's commanding presence, Becca began struggling. Unexpectedly, the man let her go. But in the same heartbeat, he grabbed an unresisting Charlie. "Make it snappy. I haven't a minute to spare!"

"Put him down!" Gram plowed ahead to intervene. Nick's warning cry came too late. Her feet parted like bookends, taking her down with a thud. Near tears himself, Nick tried to pull her up. She grimaced in pain. "Never mind about me. Give him the key, Nick."

Nick snagged the truck key from the nail just inside the baker's cabinet. The man shot a tense glance toward the basement door as the key changed hands. "Can't you shut that dog up?"

"He won't quit, not as long as you're here." Nick held out his arms to take Charlie. But Charlie, misled by the uniform, prodded the stranger's bristly chin with a dimpled finger and prattled, "Da-da?"

"Charlie, he isn't Dad! He's a thief. He's stealing Dad's truck!"

"That's enough, Nick." Gram tried to restore calm, though her face was lined with pain. "Sir, you have the key. Put the child down before you frighten him."

The man passed Charlie into Becca's outstretched arms. But relief was fleeting, for hard fingers gouged into Nick's thin shoulder.

"I can't work the pedals with this bum ankle. You'll have to drive for me."

"He'll do no such thing!" cried Gram, struggling in vain to get up.

But her protest fell on deaf ears. The man shoved Nick out the door ahead of him. Nick's heart thrashed in his chest. His throat ached as he was propelled toward the barn by the prodding hand of the burglar.

A rising moon shone through the broad door. It cast a silvery light over the truck. The man yanked the passenger door open and motioned with an impatient hand.

Nick balked. Help this criminal steal his father's truck? The truck he'd promised to care for?

"Come on, come on!" the man urged.

He couldn't do it. He couldn't let this happen. Stubbornly, Nick backed away. But the man picked him up by the shirtfront and flung him into the truck. Startled by the sudden violence, tears sprang to Nick's eyes. But he batted them back. He calmed himself with a silent prayer. Imagination, said Gram, was a good tool. An imaginative plan. A plan of escape. That's what he needed.

Closing himself in beside Nick, the man said tersely. "Start her up. Let's go!"

Nick turned the key. He pressed the starter. The engine coughed twice and caught.

"Don't turn on the lights until we're on the highway!" he warned, as Nick reached for the light lever.

Nick shifted into gear. They bounced across the dark meadow. He jerked to a stop, looked both ways, then lurched out onto the highway. In his nervousness, he let go the clutch too abruptly.

"Easy! Let the clutch go easy! Don't stray into the

76

other lane. Keep it between the lines.'' The man re-
garded oncoming headlights with growing apprehension
and put a hand on the wheel. He helped steer until the
northbound car had passed.

''I usually just drive in the meadow,'' Nick said in
a whisper.

''Driving's driving. Keep your eyes on the road, your
hands on the wheel, and your mind on what you're
doing!''

Nick shifted into third and left Sweet Clover behind.
Often he'd dreamed of motoring down Highway 66 like
a truck driver or a traveling salesman following the
winding road. But not like this! Not in the darkness
with a thief in the seat beside him. The hard road, once
so inviting, was now a cold-blooded stranger.

Or was it his fear making it unfamiliar? There were
the railroad tracks running alongside it. That was familiar. And the crossroad sign for the gravel road that ran
out to the cemetery. Though it was too dark to see, off
to the left was the sawmill. Nick grew calmer, seeing
what lay ahead in his mind. It wasn't unfamiliar at all.
The next thirty miles, he knew well. He'd ridden it
often with his father. He had to use what he knew to
his advantage.

Ahead on the right was a scenic turnout that over-
looked a green, rock-strewn valley. The graveled turnout
climbed a grassy knoll, then descended again, feeding
right back onto 66. Sometimes, when his father was
feeling his oats, he'd jerk off the highway and hit the
turnout without ever slowing. Up and over they'd fly,
past a picnic table and a garbage can, right back onto
the hard road. Invariably, Nick clutched his stomach.
''Did you lose it?'' his father would tease with a grin.

The memory encouraged Nick and reminded him of something else. The passenger door! Had it latched properly when the stranger climbed in? Did he dare try to lose the fellow on the turnout?

The thief swiveled in the seat, peering out the back window. Were they being followed? He couldn't make out any headlights. But even if Mama hadn't heard over the phone, Becca'd surely have summoned Henry Gibbs by now. Help should be coming. Hope rising, Nick tried to distract him.

"Suppose it's broken? Your ankle, I mean?" he asked.

"Keep your eyes on the road," said the man.

"Probably not. You couldn't walk on it if it was broken."

Gingerly, the man eased his foot out of the unlaced boot. Though he didn't ask for an opinion, Nick volunteered, "Pretty swollen, isn't it?"

"Hurts something fierce," the man admitted.

"You should prop it up," Nick said. "I learned that in first aid at school."

"And just how am I supposed to do that?"

"Put it up on the dashboard."

"There's no room. My leg's too long."

"Lean against the door and turn sideways."

"Just shut up and drive," the man growled. He took another tense glance over his shoulder, then turned his back to the door and elevated his foot, just as Nick had suggested.

Nick caught his breath, waiting. He was going pretty fast. Not wanting to miss the turnout, he slowed down.

"What are you doing? Are we being followed?" The man gripped the back of the seat and peered out the back window. A sparse string of twin headlights twinkled a long way behind them. "Who's back there?"

"Don't know," said Nick.

"Ought to get off this road. It's the first place they'll come looking."

"You want to take a back road?"

"Is there one close?"

"Should be. Somewhere along here." Nick squinted in the darkness, watching for landmarks. The turnout would be hard to see at night. There was a sign just short of it. It invited travelers to eat at Dottie's Café.

His headlights flitted over Dottie's sign. It was all the warning he got for the turnout. The man swore in surprise as Nick jerked hard to the right, hit the turnout, sped up the little knoll, then slammed on the brakes. The man's elevated foot rammed into the windshield. He screamed in pain and grabbed the wheel. The truck pulled hard to the right. At his captor's corrective touch, it lurched to the left, bucked back to the right just barely missing the picnic table, then skidded sideways as the turnout spilled them back onto the highway.

"Ease off the brakes—you're going to roll us over. Get off the brake!" the man shouted.

Already, it was too late. It was like watching the earth pass beneath the floor of a merry-go-round, whirling, turning, spinning out of control. Somewhere in the mayhem, Nick let go of the wheel and rolled to the floor. Thumping, squalling, screeching, scraping, grinding noises accompanied him toward oblivion.

# Eleven

———◆———

Lights shone in the darkness. Tense, anxious voices called out his name. Hands tugged at him.

"I've got you, Nick. Let go of your knees now. Straighten your legs if you can, so we can get you out of there."

The fog in Nick's head began to clear. It was Henry Gibbs's callused hand squeezing his. "There, there. You're gonna be just fine. I don't think he's hurt bad, L'Angelo. But try not to jostle him."

The railroad crossing guard, the postman, the station manager, E. Z.—one by one familiar voices penetrated the fog in Nick's head. He tried to get up. But he was trapped between the floor and the twisted dash.

"That was quick thinking, hitting the floor." E. Z.'s voice carried to him. "Probably saved you from serious injury."

Nick didn't feel "saved" at all. He smelled gasoline and cringed in alarm at the sound of wrenching metal.

"Try to relax, son. We've got to get this door pried loose before we can get you out," explained Henry.

The dark highway, the turnout, the weaving truck—
it came back in disjointed flashes. He'd driven down 66
. . . at night . . . up and over the knoll . . . too fast. He'd
rolled his father's truck! Once Henry Gibbs got him out,
he was sure to arrest him.

"He lied to me," he said, head hurting. "He isn't a
soldier! He's a thief. He stole Miss Clark's purse and
he made me drive him."

"Easy, son," Mr. Gibbs soothed. "We know all
about it. Just lie still now. It'll only be a few more
minutes."

"Where is he?" Nick asked. "Did he get away?"

"We got him. Don't you worry, everything's going
to be fine."

"How'd you find me?"

"Your sis called your mama and your mama called
me," said Mr. Gibbs.

"Iris had a part in it, too," E. Z. inserted. "She
saw the truck leave the pasture for the highway and
knew something was wrong. So she ran next door
to check."

Miss Clark! She was watching, just when it counted.
"Is Gram's arm broken?"

"Looked like it might be. Iris went to the phone
office so your mother could go home. She'll take care
of things."

Mama! She'd be mad. Dad, too, when he heard. Bitter
tears stung Nick's eyes. He wished he was little like
Charlie and could wail without shaming himself. Wail
like he was half killed. Except that he wasn't. Not unless
you counted rope-burned hands, a hummy head, and a
heavy, heavy heart.

*　　*　　*

The convoy, in Nick's absence, had bivouacked in the back pasture. Moonlight and dewdrops gilded a field of tents. Campfires burned, and the pleasant hum of quiet conversation drifted with wood smoke on the night air. But Nick, as he climbed out of Henry Gibbs's car, had little appreciation for the tranquil scene. There was Gram's busted arm and Mama's certain wrath to be faced.

The doctor's car was at the front gate, and the whole downstairs was lit up. But Mama was alone in the kitchen when the constable saw Nick to the door. Straight away, Wolf sent up a howl from the basement. Nick scarcely noticed the racket, so full was he of guilt and dread.

"Nick! My Nickie!" Much to his surprise, Mama swept him into her arms and hugged him so hard, every scrape, scratch, and bruise shouted uncle. "Thank you, thank you," she whispered prayerfully.

Nick's nose prickled. His throat swelled shut. "I'm sorry, Mama. I didn't know he was . . . b-b-bad."

"Shhh," she soothed, eyes glistening. "You're in one piece, that's what counts."

"B-but I wrecked Daddy's t-truck," he stammered.

She stiffened and held him at arm's length. "*That's* how you got all torn and scratched? Are you hurt, child? Henry, is he . . ." She turned, beseeching Constable Gibbs.

"Nothing broken. Seems to be fine." The constable shifted his hat hand to hand. "Other fella wasn't so fortunate. Knocked out cold. Busted ankle and all cut up."

"Better'n what he deserves," sputtered Mama.

"Yes, well, he'll have his say in court, ma'am. Justice can take its course."

"I don't suppose they'll be asking *me* to serve on that jury!"

"No, Maggie, I don't suppose they will." Henry Gibbs's leathery grin flashed and faded. He beckoned with his hat, asking, "That Doc's car I saw out front?"

Mama nodded. "He's tending Gram's arm."

"When he's finished with Miz Kelsey, would you have him stop by the jail and give an opinion? May have to transport my prisoner to County Hospital."

"All right, I'll tell him." One arm still wrapped around Nick, Mama added, "I don't know how to thank you for getting Nick back safe and sound."

The constable's tall frame filled the doorway. He shuffled his big feet and murmured uncomfortably, "Just doing my job."

"Yes, and doing it well, too," Mama said warmly. "Thanks again, Henry. On Rob's behalf, too. I don't know how we would have stood it if . . ."

"If, nothing. Nick's gonna be just fine." Constable Gibbs tipped his hat and excused himself, leaving Nick alone with Mama.

"Where's Becca?" he asked, for the kitchen was suddenly much too quiet.

"Upstairs with Charlie. They're watching Doc splint Gram's arm—and getting in the way, most likely."

Recognizing that flinty note creeping into her voice, Nick dropped his weary body into the nearest chair. Dropping his head, he clenched stinging hands and said miserably, "Dad's truck isn't gonna run again, Mama."

She came to stand behind him and rested her hands on his shoulders. "We'll deal with that later. Becca told

83

me about the man in the barn and how you two were caring for him. How could you keep such a dangerous secret?''

''Mama, I . . .'' Eyes swimming, he studied his shoes in triplicate. ''I thought he was a soldier.''

''So what if he was?'' she asked evenly. ''A uniform doesn't make a bad man into a good one.''

''He said he was on a secret military mission.'' Nick tried again. ''That he needed help. He made me promise not to tell.''

''So you kept your word to a stranger, even though it meant breaking the rules? Sneaking behind my back? And Gram's back?''

Nick picked at a rip in his trousers and said nothing.

''You know we don't allow anyone to sleep overnight in the barn,'' Mama said into the silence.

''Yes, but . . .''

''But what, Nick? What twisted your thinking so?''

Nick plucked at a thread, blinking back tears. ''Becca and I thought we were doing for that man what we'd want someone over there to do for Dad.''

''Oh, Nick,'' Mama murmured, all the starch going out of her. She turned his chair, knelt down in front of him, and sandwiched his rope-burned hands between hers. ''That's so good and noble-sounding. Your heart was right, but it's a boy's heart. Still tender and undiscerning.''

He lifted questioning eyes.

''Easily fooled,'' she said gently.

''Dad wouldn't have been fooled?''

''No, son. I don't think so. And someday, when you've seen how the world is, you won't be fooled by made-up stories, either. No matter how convincing.''

84

"Are you going to tell Dad?" He battled fresh tears.

She rocked back on her heels and asked with a hint of dry wit, "You think he's not going to notice?"

Nick flushed. "I *mean* are you going to write him about this?"

"No. You are."

His heart squeezed in alarm. "Mama, I can't. He said I was the man of the house."

Mama stroked his cheek. "You telling Charlie he's big enough to use the privy doesn't make it so."

"But I let Dad down. What'll he think?" Nick mumbled miserably.

"He'll think he was wrong. And he was," Mama said firmly. "You're not a man, you're a boy. A ten-year-old boy. It's not fair of him or me or anyone else to load you down with more than you can handle."

Nick looked at her in wonder. *Dad, wrong?* Who'd think of such a thing? He pondered it while she got a pan and collected warm water from the stove reservoir and a soft rag to clean his cuts and scrapes and scratches.

"Maybe I *could* have handled it, if I'd thought it through," he ventured in a timid voice.

"Mama used to tell me I had a voice inside, that I should listen and it'd keep me out of trouble," Mama said, gingerly bathing his face. "But sometimes, it's quieter than a voice. Sometimes it's just a nagging feeling that something's not quite right."

Startled, Nick blinked. He'd had that feeling. It'd grown stronger and stronger. But he just kept shoving it down.

"She'd tell me, too, that you had to know people the way they are," Mama added. "That means don't judge at face value. Scratch beneath the surface. She was right, too. I learned it the hard way when I was just about your age."

"How?" asked Nick.

Mama set in telling him then, about Uncle Jere's older brother, Bryce Bishop, how handsome and smooth-talking he was. And how once upon a time, she and her cousin Clara were so blinded by his charms they'd missed his true character.

Parts of the story were familiar to Nick. But he hadn't known Uncle Jeremiah *had* a brother, let alone a boot-legging one.

"Course we don't ever bring it up to Jere," Mama said in closing. "Even after Jere's folks died, and Bryce left him with Mama to raise, Jere put a lot of stock in his big brother."

Nick nodded understanding, warmed that after all that had happened, Mama should trust him with such a fascinating family secret.

Morning came, and because it was Sunday, the encamped soldiers stayed put. Nick watched from his window as they fell into formation and did calisthenics. A fair number of them showed up later in church. Most of the townsfolk were so busy being hospitable to the soldiers, Nick's misadventure took a backseat. Which suited him fine. He wasn't all that eager to talk about it.

Over lunch, Mama said that Miss Clark had gone to the jail just as Henry Gibbs was releasing the vagrant. Feeling bad about having falsely accused him, she gave the fellow a pair of shoes that had been her father's. She also gave him a packet of food and a few dollars to help him on his way. Reminded of Miss Clark, Nick fetched her purse from the granary and went next door to return it and thank her for sending help. But she wasn't home, so he just left the purse on her doorstep and went home to write his letter.

He settled on the porch steps. But it was a hard thing to put into words. Especially with the soldiers out in the pasture, getting ready to break camp. Becca was out there, too, making friends. Smiling and talking and dancing foot to foot while a big red-haired fellow bounced Charlie on his knee.

Nick turned as the screen door opened behind him. Mama took off her apron and sat down beside him.

"How's Gram?"

"Complaining she can't knit. But it's a clean break, Nick. Doc says it'll heal fast."

Nick took out his pocketknife and put a sharper point on his pencil.

"How's your letter coming?"

Nick read aloud from his letter, " 'Dear Dad. Gram broke her arm.' "

"And?"

"That's all I've got so far."

Mama flicked at a fly with her apron. "Take a break if you're stuck. Go on out and join Becca."

"Can't," he murmured.

"Those men get homesick, just like your daddy. They enjoy hearing a child's voice."

Nick stared at the patched knee of his trousers.

"They've got candy. Becca's stuffed chocolate until it's a wonder she's not sick," Mama tried to coax him.

"I don't want any," said Nick, though it was hard to get sweets, what with sugar being rationed.

"It's over and done, Nick. Quit brooding."

He hung his head and repeated what E. Z. had said as he passed by on the way home from church. "That uniform wasn't even his. He stole it!"

"I know."

"E. Z. says he's wanted for counterfeiting ration stamps, dealing in the black market, and armed robbery, too."

"I heard."

Nick wrote, *I wrecked your truck.* The words jumped off the page, so alarming, he crumpled up the letter and looked toward the road as a truck pulled off on the shoulder. A sailor climbed out, and started into town.

Beside him, Mama sighed. "You just never know what's passing by on this old road. It can teach a hard lesson, can't it?"

Fitting, they should call it a "hard road," thought Nick. He watched until the fellow disappeared from sight. By and by, he asked, "When do you suppose he's coming for me?"

"Who?"

"Henry Gibbs. I'm in trouble, aren't I? For driving out on the road?"

Mama's mouth wiggled. Nick's heart squeezed tight. He was sure she would cry. But to his surprise, it was a smile she was withholding. The smile soon spilled into laughter.

"If that's all that's worrying you, let me put your mind at ease. Henry Gibbs has absolutely no intentions of cluttering his jail with the likes of you!" She laughed again, then took the tablet, ordering, "Go tell your sister to quit dancing and twisting like that. I declare, she's nearly as brassy as my cousin Clara!"

Behind them, the telephone rang, two longs and a

short. Their ring. Mama patted his knee, then stood up and went to answer the phone. Nick was starting down the walk when her startled, "Who?" stopped him cold in his tracks.

"Is he all right?" Her next breathless words met him coming through the door. She was gripping the receiver tightly, listening so hard, beads of perspiration broke out on her brow.

"When?" she asked sharply, as Nick searched her face, gone suddenly pale.

"Then he's all right? You're sure he's all right?"

Noticing Nick for the first time, she turned away. But not before he saw her eyes swim.

"Thank you. Thank you so much for calling," she said, animation strengthening her voice. "I hope your husband heals quickly. We'll remember him in our prayers," she promised as the call came to an end.

"Who *was* that?" cried Nick the moment she hung up the phone.

"A Mrs. Johnson. Her husband's been fighting alongside your daddy," said Mama, eyes shining. "Seems Mr. Johnson was wounded a day ago and flown to a hospital in England."

"And he called home?" Nick interrupted.

"No. He asked a nurse to call for him and reassure his wife. Apparently, Mr. Johnson and Rob are good friends, and he wanted his wife to call us with word of your daddy, as there'd been little opportunity to get letters out. Wasn't that thoughtful?"

Knowing by her expression the news was good, Nick asked breathlessly, "How is Dad?"

Mama swept him into her arms, assuring joyously,

"Your daddy's just fine! The fighting's been rough, but thank God, he's just fine!"

Trembling with relief, Mama laughed and wiped away tears and hugged him breathless. Her relief was contagious, washing over even last night's disaster. Somehow, the mangled truck no longer seemed so devastating. His father was fine! The sun was shining. There were soldiers out there in the pasture—homesick soldiers, packing up, getting ready to leave. And Becca was getting all the chocolate!

It was evening before Nick got back to his letter. Starting was the hardest part. Finally, he just told it plain out, and as he was writing, night crept over the windowsill. Charlie toddled up to play on his bed. Mama soon followed. She heard his prayers, and led them into saying one for Mr. Johnson, too. Then she tucked Charlie into his crib, kissed them both good night, and blew out the lamp.

The house grew quiet. Nick's gaze followed the beam of a passing truck. Light spilled across his bed. It crawled up the wall, danced over Charlie, then lit the curtains on its way out.

Nick couldn't remember when his eyes had felt so heavy. He slipped under the sheet and sank into his pillow. Below in the yard, Wolf yipped, a halfhearted sound that soon faded away.

A cat, thought Nick. He yawned, closed his eyes and let the song of the hard road lull him to sleep.